W9-CUC-183

Other Books You Might Enjoy

MUDVILLE
by Kurtis Scaletta

RUMP: THE TRUE STORY OF RUMPELSTILTSKIN
by Liesl Shurtliff

THE MAGIC CAKE SHOP
by Meika Hashimoto

POWERLESS
by Matthew Cody

SAMMY KEYES AND THE NIGHT OF SKULLS
by Wendelin Van Draanen

THE BLUE SHOE
by Roderick Townley

MODERN FAIRIES, DWARVES, GOBLINS AND OTHER NASTIES
by Lesley M. M. Blume

TWO CRAFTY CRIMINALS
by Philip Pullman

SKARY CHILDRIN AND THE CAROUSEL OF SORROW
by Katy Towell

THE WEDNESDAYS

BY
JULIE BOURBEAU

ILLUSTRATED BY
JASON BEENE

A YEARLING BOOK

This is a work of fiction. Names, characters, places, and incidents
either are the product of the author's imagination or are used fictitiously.
Any resemblance to actual persons, living or dead, events, or locales
is entirely coincidental.

Text copyright © 2012 by Julie Bourbeau
Illustrations copyright © 2012 by Jason Beene

All rights reserved. Published in the United States by Yearling,
an imprint of Random House Children's Books, a division of Random
House, Inc., New York. Originally published in hardcover in the United
States by Alfred A. Knopf, an imprint of Random House Children's Books,
New York, in 2012.

Yearling and the jumping horse design
are registered trademarks of Random House, Inc.

Visit us on the Web! randomhouse.com/kids

Educators and librarians, for a variety of teaching tools,
visit us at RHTeachersLibrarians.com

The Library of Congress has cataloged the hardcover edition of this work
as follows:
Bourbeau, Julie.
The Wednesdays / by Julie Bourbeau. — 1st ed.
p. cm.
Summary: In a village where peculiar things happen every Wednesday,
one boy must save the town to save himself.
ISBN 978-0-375-86890-0 (trade) — ISBN 978-0-375-96890-7 (lib. bdg.) —
ISBN 978-0-375-89975-1 (ebook) — ISBN 978-0-375-87286-0 (pbk.)
[1. Supernatural—Fiction. 2. Villages—Fiction.] I. Title.
PZ7.B6646We 2012 [E]—dc23 2011021132

Printed in the United States of America
10 9 8 7 6 5 4 3 2 1

First Yearling Edition 2013

Random House Children's Books supports the First Amendment
and celebrates the right to read.

For Kieran,
who inspires me every day of the week

• • •

Acknowledgments

A special thank-you to my agent, Jessica Regel, for taking a chance on me when I had only the vaguest sense of what it meant to be a writer. Many thanks also to the editorial team at Knopf, especially Katherine Harrison, for catching, encouraging, and polishing until my little manuscript grew into a book. And finally, much appreciation to John Newman of the Village Clocksmith, who so patiently answered my truly weird questions about the inner workings of clock towers.

PROLOGUE

There was nothing in particular about the boy standing in the open window to indicate that he was anything other than perfectly ordinary.

But he was a boy, no denying that. And the creature staring up at him was cold and wet and unbearably grumpy, and if not *this* boy, then he'd have to keep trudging about in this blasted storm, and . . .

The boy would do just fine, he decided.

He sneezed, and then wiped his dripping nose with the back of one hairy, spidery-fingered hand. He was ready to proceed.

The steps were simple. He had but to stare at the boy and chant three short words. But he needed to stare and to chant with intensity—with feeling and with purpose, with malice and with spite.

He pushed his rain-drenched hair out of his face and narrowed his large silver eyes. *Focus.* An arrow of lightning struck the ground at his feet, causing him to smile a sharp-toothed grin. *Yes. Perfect.* The storm picked up speed, with drumbeats of thunder and brilliant slashes of lightning all around. Unaware of the danger that lurked below, the boy in the window leaned out farther to witness the beautiful fury of the storm.

Everything was in place.

"I. Choose. You." The creature's voice boomed nearly as loud as the clap of thunder that sounded at the same moment. With his mission now complete, he slunk off into the night. He'd said the words. Now it was time to wait.

CHAPTER 1

Halfway up the steep slope of Mount Tibidabo was a very small village where very strange things happened ... but only on Wednesdays.

The rest of the week was quite normal, as far as small villages in this day and age go. It was only on Wednesdays that the villagers shuttered their windows, locked their doors, and hunkered down to wait out the oddness, which always ended promptly at midnight.

In addition to being punctual, the strange Wednesday happenings were also *mostly* harmless. Oh, occasionally people stubbed their toes on a piece of furniture that was mysteriously rearranged or lost their footing on suddenly slippery surfaces; once Polly Simmons had to go to the hospital in the city to have her stomach pumped when her tea was unexpectedly switched with her perfume. But even then, Polly was all right in the end, and she later confessed that she had often thought about trying a sip of perfume just to see if it tasted as lovely as it smelled.

So, overall, it wasn't really much of a bother, and since the rest of the week in the village was pleasant enough, the people just shrugged their shoulders and stayed indoors one day out of seven.

It was on one of these Wednesdays, which started out no stranger than any other, that things started to become much, *much* stranger than usual for one boy in particular.

• • •

Max V. Bernard did *not* like to stay indoors on Wednesdays. He had no siblings to play with, since his baby brother, Leland, was too young and too ill-tempered to be any fun, and the family pet was a grumpy old cat who did nothing but sleep on the guest room bed. His mother and father spent their Wednesdays drinking lots of coffee, mopping up baby spit, and playing canasta, which in Max's opinion was truly the world's most boring card game. Max thought Wednesdays were dreadfully dull.

Because Wednesdays in the house were so boring, Max often found the need to bend the rules here and there. As far as he was concerned, being scolded was at least more interesting than playing canasta. So it was that on this particular Wednesday, he was breaking the rules by peeking out of a secret peephole. Although his father carefully sealed up the windows and doors each Tuesday night before bedtime, Max had a few tricks up his sleeve. At the moment, for example, he was hiding in the attic, where he had discovered that one of the slats in the shutters was loose and could be pried open just enough for proper spying.

Max was peering through this secret slat with wicked glee as a confused group of tourists wandered about through the center of the village. Tourists often caught the worst of the Wednesday weirdness, since they, of course, weren't aware that they really ought to be indoors. There was a large

amusement park at the top of Mount Tibidabo and a popu-
lar seaside city at the base, so it was only natural for travelers to assume that the village halfway between the two
would make for a pleasant stop. Six days out of the week
they were correct: the local cafe served lovely lunches, and
old Mr. Fife's shop displayed beautifully carved wooden butterflies that sold by the dozens to cheerful visitors.

Travelers who arrived on Wednesdays, however, always
left in a hurry—more often than not in a manner quite different from the way they had arrived.

Max watched as the group of tourists paced up and down
the street, scratching their heads in confusion as they passed
one business after another that was shuttered, locked, and
dark. The group consisted of two men, both wearing plaid
pants, two women—one of whom was enormously fat—and
one frizzy-haired teenage boy who looked every bit as bored
as Max felt. One of the men, a red-faced sort who had an
enormous camera slung around his neck, had taken it upon
himself to try to rouse the town. He marched up to the city
hall building and rapped loudly on the ornate metal door.
No one answered, of course, but he insisted on pounding
furiously on the doors of three neighboring buildings before
finally giving up. He was clearly unaware that *no one* in the
village ever answered their door on a Wednesday.

The man's face grew redder and redder as he rattled on
the doors, and the rotund woman, who Max guessed was

probably his wife, *yoo-hoo*ed and *halloo*ed shrilly. Finally, the man erupted. "What's the matter with this lunatic town? It's the middle of the day on a Wednesday—you can't just lock up the whole confounded place! I know that you can hear me!" he bellowed at no one in particular.

"We'd just like to buy some sandwiches for the road," trilled the second woman hopefully.

"And some sodas!" the teenager demanded in a sulky tone.

They were met—naturally—with silence.

Max grinned as he watched the group get into their minivan to drive away. He, of course, knew that cars rarely started on Wednesdays.

Sure enough, mere seconds later the red-faced man burst angrily from the driver's seat, this time to pound on the door and windows of the village mechanic shop. He must have been feeling defeated, though, because he gave up after only a few irritable knocks and rattles. Instead, he glumly organized his fellow travelers to push the silent car while he steered. The steep roads of Mount Tibidabo made it easy for stranded travelers to coast downhill to the city at the bottom of the mountain, and before long the car picked up speed and the unfortunate travelers hopped back in.

"*One, two, three, four . . .*" Max gleefully began to count in his head.

He never even got to five. CLANG! The car's bumper

fell off and bounced loudly on the pavement—an entirely predictable event for anyone who had lived in the village long enough. Bits and pieces fell off absolutely *everything* on Wednesdays.

Max didn't get a chance to see whether the tourists would stop to retrieve the bumper, though, because his fun was interrupted—rather abruptly—by an angry howl from downstairs.

"MAXWELL VALENTINO BERNARD! You'd better not be up there letting the wednesdays in!"

Max hastily tried to close the shutters, but it being Wednesday and all, the slat stuck and then broke off in his hand. His mother and father burst into the attic at the same time; his dad was carrying baby Leland under his arm like a football.

"You let the wednesdays in, and they made my cake fall! It's completely ruined," screeched his mother angrily.

"And they broke my television again," said his father dejectedly. "Now I'll never know who made it to the semi-finals."

Baby Leland just sneered at him.

Max felt sorry for his father, who he knew had spent the whole week looking forward to watching an important table tennis tournament on TV. But he felt sorrier for *himself* about the ruined cake. It was supposed to be *his* birthday cake, after all.

Baby Leland chose that moment to launch into his sixth screaming fit of the afternoon. He glared at Max while he howled, clearly demonstrating that he, too, thought Max was a careless nitwit.

"Oh, come to Mommy, my poor colicky little darling," Max's mother cooed, reaching for the baby. Leland settled contentedly into her arms, looked Max directly in the eyes as if to say "watch this," and then hiccuped up a torrential flood of baby spit-up.

Max and his father simultaneously stepped back, not only to avoid the mess dripping onto the floor, but also because Max's mom was growing redder and redder in the face, as if she, *too*, might erupt.

Max wrinkled his nose in disgust as he shook off a fleck of spit-up from his shoe. "Ew, yuck." They were only two thoughtless syllables, but Max's comment pushed his frazzled mother over the edge.

"That's it, Maxwell Valentino!" she bellowed, her face reaching peak redness. "I've had quite enough of your Wednesday thoughtlessness! Last week you opened the back door to let the cat out, and the week before that you opened the fireplace flue because you swore you heard an owl stuck inside. If you like the wednesdays so much, then you might as well just go outside and play with them!" She thrust baby Leland back into his father's arms with a squishy, splatting sound and then pointed down the stairs.

Max's father gasped. He seemed to be equally startled by the dramatic proclamation and the wet, smelly baby now squirming in his arms. For a moment it looked as if he was about to disagree with his wife, but then he reconsidered as he remembered that Max *had* spoiled his beloved television watching for several weeks in a row. And the fact that he was now also covered with baby spit-up did nothing at all to elevate his mood. With a sharp elbow of encouragement from Max's mother, he nodded in solemn agreement. "That's right. And don't let me hear you complaining about them turning your trousers inside out again, or crying if your bicycle tire goes flat, or . . ." He trailed off. "You'll just have to manage the wednesdays on your own," he concluded, and slunk off with baby Leland to see if, by some miracle, his television had unbroken itself.

Max sighed melodramatically as his mother marched him to the door, but he wasn't actually upset at all. He wasn't afraid of the wednesdays. It was a beautiful spring day—his birthday, no less—and he was free to roam!

His mother hesitated with her hand on the doorknob, though. "Maybe it's not such a good idea for you to go out there after all," she said, beginning to doubt her earlier haste. "Perhaps you could stay in and help me get a new cake started instead."

Max wouldn't hear of it, though; he wanted OUT. "No!

You said I could go outside!" he reminded her in a pleading tone. His mind worked quickly as he saw from his mother's expression that she remained unconvinced. "Besides, it's my birthday. Birthdays are lucky days, so the wednesdays can't do anything to me today!"

"Hmph. I sincerely doubt that, but go on with you," she relented.

She opened the door just wide enough for him to scoot out, and by the time she had pulled it shut and latched it tightly, he was already running down the front path at full steam.

CHAPTER 2

Max didn't bother with his bike—tires went flat too often on Wednesdays, and spokes tended to suffer all sorts of mishaps. Besides, the village was small, and he could walk just about anywhere he wanted to go.

He headed first for the community pool. He hadn't brought a swimsuit, but there was no one around to see him, so he simply tossed his clothes in a heap and dove in. "Swimming in my birthday suit on my birthday," he sang to himself happily as he paddled and somersaulted through the clear blue water. He found that he quite liked having the whole pool to himself for a change—there was no one to tell him to stop doing cannonballs off the edge, and there were no grumpy lap swimmers shooing him out of their lanes. He spent ages working on his backflip; it was so nice to jump off the diving platform as often as he wanted without having to wait in line!

Eventually he grew tired of swimming alone. He hadn't brought a towel with him, so he first tried shaking himself off like a dog, but that didn't quite do the trick. Luckily, he spotted a discarded towel lying crumpled up near the fence. "*Hoo*-rah!" he crowed at his good fortune. His mother would have called the towel "filthy," but Max wasn't feeling picky.

He was rubbing his head briskly with the towel when he felt something pull at his hair. "What's this?" he wondered aloud. He pulled the towel away in disgust as he realized he had just succeeded in rubbing someone's old chewing gum into his hair.

He pushed his way into the changing room to look at the damage in the mirror. It took him a few moments to find the light switch, and then the rare opportunity to swing like a monkey from locker door to locker door distracted him. When he finally got around to checking the mirror, he was startled to see that not only was his hair standing up in gummy, sticky spikes, but also that his skin was a distinct shade of pale blue.

The pool *had* seemed exceptionally blue. There must have been some sort of dye in the water, he reasoned.

"I'll get you, wednesdays!" Max yelled cheerfully. Far from being angry, he actually thought that his blue skin and spiky hair looked fantastic. He practiced several monster postures and growls in the mirror before deciding that his new appearance was more like a space alien than a monster. He stared at his reflection in the mirror for as long as he possibly could without blinking—he thought he remembered reading somewhere that space aliens didn't blink. Satisfied, he went to get dressed.

Predictably enough for a Wednesday, Max's shoes were not where he had left them. He pulled on his clothes and found a pair of cowboy boots stowed in an open locker. They were ridiculously large on him, but he quite liked the loud clomping noises they made when he walked.

He clomp-clomped back into the village square, doing his best impersonation of a blue Western space alien. He stopped in front of the pharmacy's large window to use the reflection to twist his gummy hair into one large horn on the top of his head. Pleased with the results, he spun on his heels, ready to hunt for wednesdays.

CHAPTER 3

Max decided to start looking for the wednesdays in the park. He didn't really know what to look for, but the park seemed as good a place to start as any. The cowboy boots were starting to chafe his feet a bit, so he shuffled more than he clomped. He hadn't shuffled very far into the park when he caught sight of someone sitting on a bench, facing the opposite direction.

Max snuck up behind the mystery figure as quietly as the boots would allow and then catapulted himself over the bench.

"GOTCHA!" He sprang menacingly at the bench's occupant. He realized too late that it wasn't a wednesday sitting on the bench at all—it was crazy old Mr. Grimsrud.

"Oh, I—I'm terribly sorry," Max stammered as Mr. Grimsrud leapt to his feet, grabbing at his chest with a high-pitched cry. "I didn't think anyone would be out here on a Wednesday. Except the wednesdays, you know . . ." He trailed off lamely.

Mr. Grimsrud, who looked a bit bug-eyed from the shock of being startled, huffed and puffed and dabbed at his brow for a moment before finally answering. "It's all right, young blue man. It's just that I'm not accustomed to anyone being out and about, either." He chuckled strangely and then rapped twice on the side of his head with his knuckles before settling back onto the bench.

Max had asked his mother once why Mr. Grimsrud always knocked on his head like that, but she had only shushed him and told him that the old man had had a sad life and that he shouldn't stare. That wasn't an answer at all, of course, but Max hadn't asked again.

"I'm hunting wednesdays!" Max announced. It struck him at that moment that perhaps he should find a stick or a rock or something to defend himself, just in case. He eyed Mr. Grimsrud's walking stick and wondered if he dared ask to borrow it for the hunt.

"Hunting wednesdays?" Mr. Grimsrud picked his nose pensively. "Whatever for? They've never much bothered me, you know. I don't really understand what the fuss is all about here every week. I can't even buy a tin of sardines at the corner store on Wednesdays or have a slice of pie at the cafe. The whole blasted village disappears, and I can't get a newspaper so I can do my morning crossword."

As the old man continued to fret about the weekly bothers, Max heard a rustle in the nearby shrubs. "It's a wednesday!" he cried, snatching Mr. Grimsrud's walking stick. He ran toward the sound and started whacking at the bushes.

"I say, young blue man, stop that! Stop that right now! You'll hurt him!" Mr. Grimsrud cried out.

Just in time to avoid hitting it with the stick, Max realized that the creature in the shrub wasn't a wednesday after all—it was the tiniest, ugliest dog he had ever seen. The miserable-looking animal had patchy fur, lopsided ears, a ratlike tail, and an exceptionally long tongue. The tongue dangled out the side of the poor dog's mouth and seemed to wag right along with the creature's skinny tail.

The dog sprang from the bushes and hopped onto the park bench beside Mr. Grimsrud, who patted it gently and fed it a small treat out of his pocket.

"This fine canine is Thursday," Mr. Grimsrud said, gesturing fondly toward the ugly mutt.

"Why Thursday?" Max asked.

"Because he always goes after wednesdays, of course," said Mr. Grimsrud, as if it should have been obvious to Max.

"He hunts wednesdays?" asked Max excitedly. "Has he ever caught one?"

"Oh, piffle." Mr. Grimsrud scratched behind Thursday's raggedy ear, making the dog's tongue stick out even farther. "He doesn't *really* hunt them—he just chases after them. I get the impression that he doesn't much like the way they smell."

Max had to think for a moment about whether this was useful to him or not. He decided that he'd prefer to continue the hunt on his own rather than spend any more time with the homely dog, who appeared to have a mean-looking rash on one flank. "What do they look like?" he asked.

"Who?" Mr. Grimsrud was tap-tapping on the side of his head with one hand and scratch-scratching the dog with the other.

"The wednesdays!" Max said impatiently; he was quickly becoming exasperated with the strange pair.

Mr. Grimsrud shrugged. "I've never seen one. Like I said, they don't come around near me. In fact, I sometimes suspect this entire village has gone half mad, and the people are all imagining things. Either that or they're all just a lazy bunch of no-goodniks using this wednesday nonsense as an excuse to spend the day lolling about in their knickers. I tell you, back in *my* day we didn't abide such foolishness." The old man's voice rose, and he seemed to be growing more and more agitated until he tapped lightly on his head and then began again in a calmer tone. "The only reason I think perhaps there *may* be something out there is because of how excited Thursday gets on Wednesdays."

Just as he said that, Thursday's sparse fur stood on end,

and the tiny dog bolted into the trees, barking furiously as he ran.

"See what I mean?" Mr. Grimsrud knocked on the side of his head for emphasis.

Max started after the dog, but then paused as his curiosity got the better of him. Knowing that his mother would be horrified, he turned back to the old man and asked in as polite a voice as he could possibly muster, "Why do you do that? Why do you knock on your head?"

Fortunately, Mr. Grimsrud didn't seem to mind the question a bit. "Metal plate," he answered cheerfully. "A souvenir from the war. It makes a lovely dinging sound when I tap it. Can't you hear? It sounds like the most beautiful wind chime you've ever heard. Very soothing."

Max shook his head as he darted away in the direction the dog had run. It seemed like a strange answer to him, particularly since he certainly hadn't heard any sort of sound, dinging or otherwise. He couldn't worry about it now, though—he had his first clue about where he might find the wednesdays.

He watched as Thursday darted behind a clump of trees in the distance, nearly howling in excitement. Max ran off to follow the dog, hopeful that the chase might just lead him directly to the wednesdays.

CHAPTER 4

Max crashed loudly through the tall shrubs surrounding the park, swatting his way through the prickly branches. He hoped that he wouldn't frighten the wednesdays away with all the noise, but his cowboy boots, which were becoming more and more uncomfortable by the minute, made it altogether impossible to be stealthy.

Max found Thursday sitting in the center of the vil-

lage gazebo. The large structure was normally used for public concerts and speeches, but on a Wednesday, of course, it was deserted. Thursday howled once, then lifted his leg and peed casually on the gazebo's top step.

"Stop that!" Max said sternly

to the dog. "Show some manners. Now shoo. I'm busy here. Get going!"

The dog trotted off reluctantly, and Max decided to have a look around. He climbed the gazebo stairs, carefully stepping over the wet spot left behind by the dog. Suddenly, the hairs on the back of his neck stood up. Although he couldn't explain it, he felt quite certain that the wednesdays were nearby. He crouched quietly in the gazebo for a moment, but he didn't hear anything at all—even the birds seemed to have stopped singing.

Max realized he still had Mr. Grimsrud's walking stick in his hand. He hadn't intended to run off with it, but now he tightened his grip on it gratefully. He didn't *think* the wednesdays were dangerous, at least not in a bite-your-finger-off sort of way, but he really didn't know enough about them to be sure. He *did* know, however, that whatever they were, they were frightening enough to make all of the grown-ups in the village lock their doors and stay inside each and every Wednesday. Even big Bill Kraussen, their next-door neighbor, who had been a professional wrestler for years, refused to set foot out of his house on a Wednesday. The wednesdays must be at least *somewhat* dangerous, reasoned Max, if a man like big Bill was afraid of them.

Still, he couldn't help himself. He just wanted to *see* one. He began to wish that he was wearing his comfortable sneakers instead of the cowboy boots, since he didn't know how fast he'd be able to run in the boots. Not that he planned to run away, but still—always best to be prepared.

He attempted to tiptoe silently down the stairs, but the boots were too stiff. He winced with every CLOMP on each wooden step. With the amount of noise he was making, he was practically *inviting* the wednesdays to come do whatever it was that they did to him.

Safely back on quieter soil, Max crept around the perimeter of the gazebo. The eerie silence was making him jumpy, so he started to sing quietly under his breath. "Where are you, wily wednesday? I'm weary of your wicked work. I'm waging war on wednesdays, and soon we'll all . . ."

He was struggling to come up with more words that began with W when, out of the corner of his eye, he saw something dart under the stairs.

He pounced immediately, no longer caring whether his boots made noise. "I see you, wednesday! Come out of there, right now!" He poked the walking stick through the space between the stairs, jabbing blindly at whatever was under there. It occurred to him—briefly—that he might hurt the thing. He poked again, slightly gentler than before.

Nothing happened.

Max took a step back to ponder his next move. He *knew* that he had seen something, and his skin was positively crawling. It *had* to be a wednesday.

But he wasn't sure that he wanted to crawl underneath the gazebo to find out for certain.

He weighed his options carefully. On the one hand, whatever it was that had squeezed under the stairs couldn't be too terribly enormous, or it never would have fit into the small crawl space. On the other hand, even small things could certainly be dangerous. He wondered, for the first time, whether wednesdays had teeth.

Max had grown up hearing about the wednesdays, of course. Everyone in the village knew there was *something* that caused all sorts of problems and mishaps once a week and that it was best to stay locked up inside. But, come to think of it, he had never heard anyone talk about actually *seeing* a wednesday. Big or small, fanged or not, no one really knew, since everyone just generally avoided them.

I'll be the first to see one! The very thought was enough to erase any lingering fears. He crouched down, took a small step closer, and peered through the space between the steps.

There was definitely something under there.

A set of large, silvery eyes was staring back at him.

Max leapt backward, only barely keeping his balance. "Aaahh!" he shrieked in a decidedly less-than-courageous pitch.

The wednesday darted back out of sight, and Max realized he hadn't even managed to get a good look at the thing. Were those sharp teeth that he had seen? Did it have talons?

A tail? His imagination began to fill in where his eyes had failed him. All thoughts of gentleness vanished from his mind, and he jabbed his stick frantically at the thing under the stairs. He had no intention of letting any sort of monster get the upper hand—or upper claw, as the case might be— even if it was smaller than him. "Out, you . . . you thing!" He gripped his stick like a spear and lunged.

But mid-lunge, Max felt his feet slip out from underneath him as if he had stepped on marbles. He lost his balance and tumbled roughly to the ground, losing his grip on the walking stick as he fell. He had jumped to his feet quickly, ready to attack again, when something flew into his mouth.

"Yuck!" Max spit and spit, but he could tell he had already swallowed whatever insect it was that had decided to take a tour of his tonsils. He coughed uselessly, disgusted.

"Yuck!" a voice that sounded an awful lot like his own cried out, almost as if there was a much-delayed echo. A high-pitched giggle sounded from under the gazebo.

The wednesday was mocking him.

"That's not funny!" yelled Max angrily. "Come out of there!"

The silvery eyes blinked calmly.

Max decided to try a new approach. He dusted himself off and then, using the calmest voice he could muster, asked, "Are you the wednesday?"

There was a long silence. Finally, a whispery voice responded. "I'm *a* wednesday, same as all of us."

Max whirled around, half expecting to be surrounded by silvery-eyed creatures. No one—or *nothing*—else was in sight, though. "Are there more of you under there?" he asked, his voice quavering just slightly. He inched slowly to his right, hoping to grab the cane before anyone else decided to join them.

But just when he was close enough to reach down for his walking stick, the thing under the stairs flew out, heading directly for him.

CHAPTER 5

Max ducked, instinctively shielding his face with his arms as the wednesday leapt out from under the stairs as if propelled by springs. The thing under the stairs popped to its feet and leered at Max, like a nightmare version of baby Leland's windup jack-in-the-box.

The creature bounced from side to side, moving remarkably fast, and its silver eyes had a sort of hypnotic quality to them that made Max feel slightly off balance. Looking at the wednesday's eyes was almost like looking into a mirror. They weren't *actually* reflective, but they were just silvery and shiny enough that you couldn't help but search for your reflection in them.

Besides the silver eyes, the wednesday appeared more or less boylike, in a crooked, simultaneously squished-down, stretched-out sort of way. It looked like a proper boy whose arms had been pulled like taffy, while the rest of his body had been scrunched down into a tubby egg shape with springy, squat legs. Max was relieved to see that he was at least a foot taller than the thing that bounced around him.

The creature's head was mostly head-shaped and -sized, except for the fact that it seemed vaguely square and didn't appear to have the benefit of much of a neck to sit upon. Overall, the thing gave the impression of being rather putty-like. In fact, as Max watched, the wednesday crept backward and squidged itself into the corner formed by the stairs against the gazebo. Once there, the creature blended into the space until it was almost invisible—all except for its large, slowly blinking silver eyes.

Once Max got over the shock that he had received when the wednesday jumped out at him, he realized that it didn't look very scary or even very monster-ish at all. It didn't have any fangs or claws, for starters, and huddled in the corner like that, it almost looked frightened. Max began to feel slightly sheepish. Monster or not, he hadn't been very polite to the wednesday.

"I won't hurt you," Max said gently, although he once again inched slightly closer to the walking stick on the ground as he spoke.

The creature giggled softly, and then a tree branch fell out of the tree and knocked Max soundly on the head.

"Hey!" Max protested, rubbing the spot where the branch had struck. "That could have really hurt me." He hadn't actually *seen* the wednesday do anything to cause the branch to fall, but Max knew a guilty expression when he saw one, and the bouncing, giggling thing that stood before him *definitely* looked guilty. "Why did you have to go and do that?"

"I didn't *really* do it," replied the wednesday, who was grinning a mocking, taunting sort of grin. Perhaps that was just the way a wednesday looked when it smiled, but Max didn't appreciate it either way.

"You did so! You were looking right at me, and then you laughed, and then the branch hit me!" Max thought it was awfully cowardly that the wednesday wouldn't at least *admit* he had made the branch fall. But the wednesday just shook his corner-shaped head and giggled again.

Max decided to attempt a different approach. "What's your name?" He tried very hard not to so much as look in the direction of his walking stick.

The silvery eyes blinked and rippled. "Ninety-eight."

"Ninety-eight? That's not a name—it's a number!" Max protested. He was almost certain that the wednesday was trying to annoy him on purpose.

"It's better than *your* name," the boylike creature said, and then giggled in what Max was starting to think was not a very nice way at all.

"You don't even know my name; I haven't told you!" Max started to argue, but the wednesday suddenly darted out of the corner and headed off toward the woods.

"Of course I know your name. It's Next." Not having much of a neck to speak of, the wednesday had to pivot around to call back to Max. The creature beckoned for Max to follow him as he started walking on his squat, bouncy legs toward the trees.

"It's *Max*, not Next!" Max shouted, but the wednesday didn't respond. Max shrugged and decided to follow. He was quite certain this would all turn out to be either a very good or a very bad idea. He just wished that he could tell which one.

• • •

Max followed the wednesday through a thicket of trees, across the park playground, and behind the village grocery store. He looked for Mr. Grimsrud as they passed by the bench where he had been sitting, but apparently the old man had already left the park. Max was disappointed—he had wanted someone else to see the wednesday he was following, if only to prove that he wasn't imagining things. Not that the crazy old man would be his first choice as a witness, but it wasn't as if anyone else in the village was likely to be walking about on this day of the week. Besides, he felt guilty for running off with Mr. Grimsrud's walking stick. He'd have to return it later, though—right now he needed to keep up with the creature that was skittering and bouncing along a few paces ahead.

The wednesday finally stopped near a Dumpster behind the store, and then sort of faded into the corner where the bin met the back of the building. Max could still see him, but just barely.

Max tensed, not knowing what to expect. There was no sound at all—even the wind seemed to be holding its breath. His eyes scanned left and right, searching for wednesdays. There were an awful lot of hiding places in this particular spot. Between the tall weeds, the thick bushes, the stacked cartons, and the parked delivery trucks, there must have been dozens of places where a wednesday could lie in wait.

"What's going on?" he finally yelled when he couldn't stand it any longer. "Why did you lead me here?"

The silence continued.

"Come out!" Max shouted again, struggling briefly between fright and annoyance. A giggle from the corner where Ninety-eight—as if that was any sort of a name—had hidden pushed away the fear, though. Nothing dangerous could possibly have such an irritating laugh. He clomped over to a large box and kicked it as hard as he could.

The empty box fell over but revealed nothing—or no one.

He was about to stomp away in disgust when a quick glint of silver caught his eye. There was another, then another, then another. There were dozens and dozens of sets of silver eyes staring at him—they were everywhere! Mirror-like eyes blinked at him from underneath every parked car, behind every tree, and from every corner, alley, and doorway of the surrounding buildings. Max turned around very slowly, confirming that—just as he suspected—he was surrounded by an entire army of wednesdays.

CHAPTER 6

Max might have been surrounded, but he also had gum in his hair and blisters on his feet, and he was starting to feel very cross.

"Which one of you guttersnipes turned me blue?" he demanded in his gruffest, sternest voice. He didn't know exactly what the word *guttersnipe* meant, but he had often heard the school principal use it, and he thought it sounded commanding and grown-up.

One of the wednesdays giggled stupidly.

Max spun around angrily. "Keep quiet, Ninety-eight, you bothersome little square-headed goblin!"

The silver eyes all seemed to widen at once, and dozens of whispery voices twittered words that Max couldn't quite make out.

"I'm not a goblin," said a voice from the corner where Max

had last seen Ninety-eight. The voice sounded genuinely hurt. "And it wasn't me that laughed. It was Seventy-three."

"Tattletale!" shouted a voice that sounded just like Ninety-eight's but came from behind a truck parked on the opposite side of the clearing.

Giggles and whispers erupted all around.

"Show yourselves!" Max thundered as he picked up a rock from the ground and threw it at a cluster of silver eyes.

To his amazement, the rock bounced back at him as if he had thrown it against some sort of invisible barrier. "Ow," he cried as it struck his shin—not because it had actually hurt, but because he was so startled.

There were more giggles, and then a slight rustling sound as dozens of wednesdays began to emerge out of every nook and cranny.

They all looked more or less the same. Some were slightly taller and some were slightly fatter than others, but they all had the same silvery eyes and the same long, bendy arms and vaguely corner-shaped heads. And they all giggled incessantly.

"Shut up, all of you!" demanded Max, who was by now truly and thoroughly annoyed.

Surprisingly, they did. But silent, they were creepier than when they were laughing at him. They had a way of narrowing their silver eyes until they looked like daggers, and Max definitely did not like the way they were closing in around him. He raised his fists and stood in what he believed to be a boxer's stance—not that he knew how to box, but it made him feel more prepared all the same.

The creatures silently formed a ring around him.

Max lunged at one of the wednesdays—except for their strangely long arms, he was bigger and taller than they were, so he thought he might be able to at least put a good scare in one or two of them. But either the ill-fitting cowboy boots or the fact that it was a Wednesday made him trip over his own feet and fall in a clumsy heap.

As he untangled himself from his fall, the wednesdays moved in closer and started to whisper. It took Max a few moments to sort out their strange, slithery voices, but he realized that they were *chanting* something.

"Don't you cast a wednesday spell on me!" he warned, but the creatures paid no attention. They started swaying and moving slowly in a circle as they chanted.

Max couldn't make out all the words at first, but after they had repeated themselves a few times, he started to pick up on parts of their chant:

Chaos, mayhem, plain bad luck.
One day a week we run amok.

He caught a few other words here and there, but they didn't make much sense, and he couldn't figure out the rest of the rhyme.

Max sat fuming in the dirt, surrounded by the loathsome, chanting creatures. Feeling powerless and terribly frustrated, he resorted to something he knew he was far too old for: he stuck his tongue out at the wednesdays and then pushed his nose up with his fingers to make a hideous pig monster face.

The chanting stopped immediately.

Much to Max's surprise, making a silly face had an enormous impact on the wednesdays. They squealed and jumped in delight, mimicking his expression.

When Max realized they were copying him, he growled at the wednesdays and then barked at them like a dog.

The wednesdays barked back in glee.

Max grinned, stood up, dusted himself off, and then did a handstand. It had taken him months of practice to learn how; he was certain that the wednesdays wouldn't be able to copy him.

Sure enough, the wednesdays struggled with the handstand. Their long, bendy arms weren't good for supporting their squat bodies, and they kept collapsing into tangled heaps in the dirt.

Soon Max was giggling just as much as the creatures. He crouched down, made horns with his fingers, and then sprang upward yelling, "Booga-booga-booga!"

The wednesdays loved this one. Some of them started adding their own touches, like a spin during the leap or an extra *ooga* tacked on to the *booga*s.

Max paused. He wanted to come up with something *really* challenging for his next act. He glanced around, looking for something to leap from. He eyed the closed Dumpster, which stood between an empty wooden crate on one side and a tall pile of raked leaves on the other. *Perfect.* If he could manage to vault from the crate to the top of the Dumpster, he could then take a spectacular flying leap into the leaves. The only tricky part was that he had to break through the tight circle of wednesdays in order to jump onto the Dumpster.

Max waited for just the right moment. Finally, a gap appeared between two of the smaller wednesdays, who were cackling and skipping as they made hideous faces at one another. Max took advantage of their distraction to dash through the space between the two creatures. He hopped onto the crate and then leapt with all of his might to get to the top of the Dumpster. The Dumpster that he was *quite* certain had been firmly closed.

Only, when he landed, instead of launching immediately from the Dumpster lid to the pile of leaves, he found himself plunging down into a stinking, wet, vaguely warm pile of rotting grocery store refuse. The Dumpster lid, which had mysteriously opened in the split second between Max's leap and his landing, crashed down, leaving him surrounded by foul, putrid darkness.

"Ew, disgusting!" yelled Max, his stomach lurching from

the smell of spoiled sausages and sour milk. "Very funny, everyone. You can let me out now!"

Max fully expected to see the silly, grinning wednesdays open up the lid of the Dumpster, but none appeared. He banged on the metal wall closest to him, pulling his hand back in disgust as it made contact with something even wetter and squishier than the rest of the rotting garbage around him.

He couldn't hear anything at all. No chanting, no giggling, no leaping, no voices. Was this one of their wednesday tricks?

He had sunk to the bottom of the loosely packed garbage by now; to reach the lid of the Dumpster he had to scramble up through unspeakably smelly objects that he was very glad he couldn't identify in the dark. Cartons and containers burst and leaked under his feet, and his hands clawed through plastic-wrapped horrors as he tried to reach the lid. Finally, he managed to climb high enough to push up against the roof of the bin. It wouldn't budge.

Max shifted his weight to get in a better position to push upward, but the lid still held firm.

He was trapped.

CHAPTER 7

Fortunately, Max was not one to panic.

He did, however, want out, and he wanted out NOW. It was smelly, dark, and damp in the Dumpster, and it suddenly occurred to him that this was a truly terrible way to spend one's birthday.

"This isn't funny anymore!" he shouted to the wednesdays. He pounded furiously on the sides of the container, cringing each time his hands struck some unidentifiable filth.

Finally, he heard something.

It wasn't a wednesday noise, though. It was the far more welcome sound of a small dog barking.

"Thursday! Mr. Grimsrud! Anyone! Please help me, I'm in the Dumpster!" he yelled at the top of his lungs, pounding and kicking at the metal sides.

It seemed as if an eternity passed before the lid finally began to lift. Max pushed his way out frantically, gratefully gasping the fresh air.

Mr. Grimsrud wrinkled his nose. "Young man, now you're blue *and* you smell dreadful."

Max thanked the old man profusely for rescuing him as he plucked putrid gobs from his hair and did his best to rub away some of the slimy strands stuck to his face. "Did you see them? Did you see the wednesdays? Aren't they incredible? Where did they go? Did your dog catch one?"

"Settle down, lad. Take a deep breath. Well, on second thought, perhaps you shouldn't do that considering how terrible you smell." Mr. Grimsrud fanned the air in front of his face and then knocked twice on the side of his head. "The only thing I saw was Thursday sniffing the air and then running in this direction as if his little life depended on it. By the time I got here, there was nothing but the sound of you yelling for help. I probably would've sniffed you out, too, if I'd had a moment. Phew!"

Max was disappointed. How could the wednesdays have disappeared so quickly? What had happened?

He tried to explain to Mr. Grimsrud. "I was playing with the wednesdays. They were all here—dozens of them—dancing in a big circle and chanting things. We were making faces, and then I think maybe they thought I was trying to escape, because they locked me in here after I jumped. . . ."

Mr. Grimsrud waved off Max's explanation. "You're not making any sense, lad. But I want to take a bath just looking at you, and that says a lot, since I don't much care for bathing. Is that creamed spinach on your shirt?"

Max did his best to wipe off the rotten food still clinging to his clothing. "Never mind. If you didn't see them, then I guess it doesn't matter. Thanks again for rescuing me. Sorry about your walking stick." He sighed as he handed the cane, which was now slightly sticky with something that felt like maple syrup, back to Mr. Grimsrud. He waved farewell and then headed toward home. At least he had birthday cake to look forward to there.

● ● ●

The walk home took longer than usual because by now the cowboy boots had given Max painful blisters on both feet. To make matters worse, he could tell by the CLOMP-SQUISH sound of every step that they were filled with rotten food. He sat down on the sidewalk and pulled the boots off, grimacing at the egg yolk coating one of his socks and the curdled yogurt on the other. He tossed the ruined boots in a trash can with a silent apology to whoever they had belonged to and walked the rest of the way home in his bare feet.

His parents were sitting at the table playing canasta when he walked into the house.

"MAXWELL!" his mother shrieked when she saw him. She jumped up out of her chair, startling baby Leland, who had been napping in a bassinet. "What on earth?"

The baby's face started to pinch and contort as he worked himself up into a good loud scream.

Max's father stayed seated, grimly shaking his head. "I told you we shouldn't have sent him out on a Wednesday," he said reproachfully. "And we'd just gone nearly a full ten minutes without the baby crying."

"Oh, but it's not usually *this* bad on a Wednesday," Max's mother protested weakly. "At least not indoors. Max, what is that in your hair? What is that smell? And why are you BLUE?" For a moment she looked as if she was going to faint.

"Don't worry, I'm fine," Max said bravely. "I just need a quick bath."

"I'm not so sure about the quick part," said his father, holding his nose and shooing Max toward the bathroom. "You'd do well to spend a good long time scrubbing at that mess. Besides, you've frightened your little brother coming in looking like that. Just listen to how you've made him cry."

Max resisted the urge to tell his dad that *everything* made

Leland cry. As he closed the door to run a bath he heard his mother say that she hoped none of the neighbors had seen him come home looking that way. "They'll think I'm the worst mother in the village for sending him out there on a Wednesday," she wailed as his father hugged her, shushing her gently.

Max ran the bathwater as hot as he could stand it. He scrubbed and scrubbed until both the blue dye and the smell were finally gone; his skin felt raw and chafed as he toweled himself dry. He saw that he had left a slight blue ring around the tub, but he was far too tired to do anything about it just then.

Upstairs in his room, he changed into his pajamas even though it was still early; he didn't think anyone could possibly object to him eating his birthday dinner in his pj's.

When he walked downstairs, his parents abruptly stopped their conversation and stood up quickly with large, nervous smiles on both of their faces.

"Darling," started his mother. "We feel just awful for sending you out there, especially on your birthday. It wasn't too terribly unpleasant, was it?"

"Come, Max. Sit here. Your mother has cooked your favorite meal." His father pulled his chair out for him, at the same time plunking baby Leland into his high chair.

Max sat, and then thought for a moment before answering.

The afternoon might have ended badly, but on the whole, it had been quite an adventure. "Actually, it wasn't terrible at all. I met the wednesdays! They're strange and tricky, and they have the oddest silver eyes, but they're really a lot of fun to play with."

His parents both gasped. Now his mother *really* looked as if she was going to faint. "You . . . *met* the wednesdays?" his father stammered. "What do you mean by that?"

His mother moaned and covered her face with her hands.

"No, no, don't get all upset like that." Max tried to reassure them. "Really, it was fine. They danced and chanted and we made funny faces at each other." He tried to explain what had happened, but his parents just looked pale.

"Well, at least it's over," said his mother finally. She looked uncomfortable, as if she would rather be discussing *anything* other than the wednesdays. "That's enough of this nonsense, and dinner is getting cold. Let's eat so we can have birthday cake and presents afterward."

• • •

His mother might have prepared his favorite foods and baked not one, but *two* cakes that day, but Max's birthday dinner did *not* go well at all.

First the lights went out in the dining room. "Candlelight is nicer anyway," said his father nervously after the replacement lightbulb also went dark.

Then they discovered that the saltshaker had been filled with sugar. "That's okay. Spaghetti sauce is still good when it's a little sweet," his mother said anxiously.

Then the leg on Max's chair snapped, sending him tumbling to the floor. "I was tipping back on it," he apologized as he moved to the spare chair, even though he hadn't been tipping back at all.

Finally, it was time for dessert. Max's mother and father came out of the kitchen with his birthday cake covered in brightly flaming candles, singing, "Happy birthday to you, happy birthday to you. Happy birthday, dear Maxwell . . ."

"Mom! Look out!" Max shouted as the ends of her hair brushed against one of the candles and burst into flame.

His father reacted quickly, picking up the pitcher of fresh-squeezed lemonade from the table and dumping it over his mother's flaming head.

All three of them stood in silence, Max cringing as he watched his mother and the cake both dripping lemonade and runny frosting onto the floor. Even baby Leland stopped his constant fussing for once. He sat quietly in his high chair and stared at Max in a most peculiar way.

Max's mother finally broke the long silence. "Max, darling," she whispered, looking bedraggled and very, very sad. "I think you've caught a case of the wednesdays."

CHAPTER 8

Several more unfortunate incidents in a short time span convinced the Bernard family that their suspicion was correct. Max had most definitely caught a case of the wednesdays. None of them had ever actually heard of such a thing, but it was the only explanation for an evening that ended with a small flood in the basement, a very angry cat with singed whiskers, baby Leland's blankie in tatters, and Max's mother in tears.

"Son, perhaps it would be best if you slept in your tree house tonight?" Max's father prompted gently as he passed a second and then a third tissue to his wife. She used one to dry her eyes and two to mop up the puddle of baby spit-up from her lap. "I could even join you. It'd be like a campout."

"Sure, Dad." Max tried his hardest to sound cheerful, but he knew he wasn't convincing. "Mom, don't cry. It'll be midnight in a few hours, and I'm sure everything will be better tomorrow. It's just a Wednesday thing."

"I'm sure you're right, darling." His mother's attempt to sound cheerful wasn't convincing, either.

Max pulled his sleeping bag and some extra blankets out of his closet, but he told his dad that he'd prefer to sleep alone outside. "It's nice of you to offer, really, but I think I'd like to be alone for a little while. Just to, you know, think about things a bit. And maybe instead of the tree house, I'll just set up my tent in the backyard." Max didn't even want to think about the terrible things that could go wrong ten feet up in a tree.

Max and his father set up the tent with only a few minor mishaps and accidents. He kissed his mother good night, and then wearily zipped himself into the pup tent.

• • •

Max slept surprisingly well, all things considered. Back in the house, baby Leland was in the habit of waking the entire family two or three times a night with his wailing. In contrast, the backyard was refreshingly quiet and peaceful.

The next morning, his mother woke him up with a mug of hot cocoa and a freshly baked muffin. Unlike Max, she did *not* look as if she'd had a good night's sleep.

She set the tray down *very* carefully and backed away slowly to watch. Max gingerly lifted the mug and took a cautious sip. Then he took a slow nibble, and waited.

His mother appeared to be holding her breath.

Thirty seconds went by, and then a minute. Finally, Max grinned. "It's good!" he announced. "No spills, no burns, and no chipped teeth!"

"Oh, thank goodness!" cried his mother, swooping in for a hug.

"Happy Thursday!" they both sang out.

Max hadn't wanted to admit it to himself, but he had been awfully worried. As far as he could tell, coming down with a case of the wednesdays meant being generally unlucky, breaking lots of things around the house without meaning to, and making your mother cry a lot. He'd much rather have chicken pox or even the stomach flu than a case of the wednesdays, he decided. The fact that Thursday came and went without a single incident made him feel loads happier. And when the rest of the week proved to be quite good, all around, he concluded that the whole thing must have been a silly misunderstanding.

Although he felt certain that his bout of the wednesdays was over, he still told only one of his schoolmates about meeting the creatures. Noah was his best friend, and therefore presumably more likely to believe him than anyone else. He didn't want to risk telling anybody else until he understood what had happened a little better. Or until he had proof.

Noah's reaction was to punch Max on the arm. Twice. "Yeah, right! And did you see any flying saucers while you were at it? Or maybe a talking rabbit?"

Max rubbed his arm. "Ow, stop. I did see them, I swear it!"

"Well, then, you've either gone completely crazy, or . . ." He paused, thinking. "Nope, that's the only possibility. You've gone mad. Bonkers, off your trolley, foaming at the mouth, loony tunes, insane." He punched Max's arm one more time for good measure. "Just please tell me that the fact that you're now a certifiable lunatic won't stop you from playing soccer after school today?"

Nothing Max said could convince Noah he was telling the truth.

"All right, I'll prove it to you," he said finally.

Noah crossed his arms and raised an eyebrow. "How?"

"Listen for a tap at your bedroom window next Wednesday. Open up when you hear it."

This got Noah's attention. "Nooooo . . . Really? But . . ." For once, he was speechless.

Max grinned, feeling oddly proud. "Unless you're scared, of course." He returned one of Noah's arm punches, but Noah didn't even seem to notice.

"If you're lying . . . ," Noah said, doing his best to sound threatening. Though with his round, freckled face and ever-present grin, threatening was not a quality Noah pulled off easily.

"Just open the window," Max promised.

Now he just needed to come up with a plan to show Noah the wednesdays. He could hardly wait.

• • •

His parents did not like his plan one bit.

"Maxwell Valentino Bernard, I absolutely forbid it!" His mother stomped her foot and crossed her arms. "You are NOT leaving this house tomorrow."

It was Tuesday night, and his plans were falling apart.

First, his father refused to let him use the family video camera. "They've broken my television set more times than I can count, and let's not even talk about what they've done to my car. That video camera is practically brand-new, and I'm not letting it go anywhere near the wednesdays."

Max knew that without video evidence of the wednesdays, Noah wouldn't be the only one accusing him of being a liar. Theirs was a small village, and nothing stayed secret for long. Besides his parents, both Noah and Mr. Grimsrud knew about Max's encounter. Someone, at some point, was sure to let something slip. And once word got out about his Wednesday adventures, the other villagers were sure to wonder if he was telling the truth. If Max wanted anyone to believe his story, he was going to have to get creative.

His mother, however, would not compromise on *any* of his ideas. "You will stay in this house all day long," she insisted. "No windows, no doors, no peeking out curtains."

Nothing Max said would make her budge.

Max went to bed frustrated. He spent most of the night coming up with new arguments to use to convince his parents. He *had* to get his proof.

In the morning, though, his arguments all became unnecessary.

His case of the wednesdays was back.

CHAPTER 9

Max's mother gripped his shoulder tightly as she marched him across the village square. Her hair dryer had gone on the fritz that morning, so half her hair looked smooth and dry while the rest was matted damply to her skull. Her eyes darted nervously from side to side, and she was walking so fast that Max almost had to run to keep up with her.

"Do you see them?" she hissed. One of her contact lenses had fallen—or rather *leapt,* as she shakily claimed—into a pan of scrambled eggs that morning, and she was having trouble seeing straight.

Max shook his head. He hadn't seen any sign of the wednesdays yet, but they had only been walking for two blocks.

"Here we are," his mother announced. She banged loudly on the door of the doctor's office.

"But, Mom, it's Wednesday. He won't be at work today," Max protested.

"That may be true, but he lives upstairs, so we'll just have to make enough noise to get him to come to work." She picked up a handful of pebbles and began tossing them at the second-story window. The curtains didn't so much as flutter.

She handed Max some of the pebbles and gestured for him to throw them at the window, too.

Whether it was because it was a Wednesday or whether it would have happened anyway was unclear, but Max's first pebble hit the windowpane dead center and caused a spider-web of cracks to appear.

The curtains were yanked open immediately.

"Are you people completely insane?" Dr. Tetley's face was scarlet as he opened the window to shout down to them. "It's Wednesday!"

"I'm very sorry, but we have a bit of an emergency. Max seems to have come down with a slight case of the wednes-days," Max's mother called out hopefully.

The color drained from Dr. Tetley's face, and he slammed the window shut so hard that the cracks marring the glass grew even worse.

The doctor appeared to be trying to speak to them through the closed window, but they couldn't hear what he was saying. Max's mother promptly picked up a much larger rock than the one that had cracked the window and gestured to the doctor that she intended to throw it.

"Wait!" the doctor mouthed, and then pointed downstairs.

"I'll do it. I'll break his lousy window if he doesn't help us," growled his mother.

Max was a little bit impressed, and also slightly intimidated by this new side of his mother. He did not doubt her threat at all.

Fortunately, Dr. Tetley soon appeared at the glass door of the medical office, holding a mug of coffee in both hands as if it were a shield protecting him from Max. He refused to open the door. "This will be fine." He bent down and called through the mail slot. "We can take turns speaking through here."

Max's mother sighed, but kneeled down and began a hurried conversation with the doctor through the slot.

Max wandered off while the grown-ups spoke. He could tell that he was making Dr. Tetley nervous, and besides, he wanted to look for the wednesdays.

He looked up and down the deserted streets, but he didn't see any trace of them. He thought about calling out to them, but he didn't really know what to say. "Here, wednesdays, c'mere, little fellas," he finally called in the same way that he called the cat when it wandered off outside. Nothing—or no one—responded, though.

Bored, he headed back to the doctor's office. His mother was bent at the waist, shouting into the door slot. "This is absolutely unacceptable! We can't possibly wait that long!" She sounded furious.

As Max got closer, two things happened at the same time: the handle broke off Dr. Tetley's coffee mug, causing hot coffee to spill all over his shirt, and a great big dollop of bird poop landed in his mom's hair. Dr. Tetley looked terrified, and he scuttled backward away from Max, even though the glass door still separated them. Max's mother sighed and pulled a tissue out of her purse. "Not again," she moaned quietly.

It was the third time since they had left the house that morning that a bird had scored a direct hit on her.

"Sorry, Mom," Max whispered, and took a few steps back. He wished he knew how far away from her he'd have to stand to keep from bringing her bad luck.

"We're almost done here, darling." She turned back toward the doctor and her tone hardened. "Well, at least tell me whether it's contagious."

His voice was muffled, since he now refused to even come close enough to Max to open the mail slot. "I don't know, and I don't wish to find out. You'll just have to wait until the specialist comes. Good luck to you." With that, he hurried away upstairs. Max was pleased to see as the doctor turned around that his pants had split wide open.

"Well done, dear." His mother had seen Dr. Tetley's pants, too. "That man is simply not helpful at all. He says he can't get a specialist here until the end of the week."

"I didn't mean to do it," protested Max. But he felt a tad confused. It was true that he hadn't intentionally broken the doctor's window or split his pants, but a part of him wondered if he could somehow be responsible. The only way he could describe it was that it just wasn't a *surprise* when those things occurred—as if somewhere, deep in his brain, he already knew they were going to happen.

Dr. Tetley was no help at all, and the specialist wouldn't be there for days. Max knew that the only way he could learn more about his case of the wednesdays was to go out and simply ask the wednesdays himself.

"Mom." He tugged at her sleeve. "Let me go out and play. It's going to be like this all day." Another bird plop landed on his mother's shoe.

"Oh, dear. I'm out of tissues." She looked as if she was going to cry.

"Besides"—Max could tell she was starting to waver—"don't you have to go home to take care of baby Leland's hair?" Somehow, during the course of the unusually chaotic morning, Leland had coated himself from head to toe in black shoe polish. Most of it had washed off his skin (although his complexion was still a bit on the grayish side), but no amount of shampoo or scrubbing could remove it from his previously light blond hair. With his new, shiny black waves, Max thought he looked a bit like a baby Elvis.

"My poor little cherub." Max's mother sighed. "His beautiful golden curls are ruined!" Now she started to sob in earnest.

"I'll be fine by myself," he reassured her, patting her hand sympathetically. "The baby needs you." That one always did the trick, he knew.

She finally relented, but she insisted that he ring the doorbell at their house at least once every two hours to let her know he was all right.

"And stay away from those awful wednesdays!" she called out tearfully as Max ran off.

Max pretended that he hadn't heard her. He had every intention of finding the wednesdays. After a quick stop, that was.

CHAPTER 10

Max crept around to the side of the sprawling brick house and tapped lightly on the third window on the first floor. It was Wednesday, so the window was shuttered, of course. Since he couldn't see in, Max could only hope that Noah was alone inside his bedroom. He had two dreadfully screechy older sisters who Max *definitely* didn't want to run into today.

For once, luck was on Max's side. The shutters snapped open to reveal Noah's wide eyes.

"Hiya!" Max waved cheerfully.

Noah tilted his head and frowned, rubbing sleep from one eye. "Wait a minute. Isn't it . . . ?"

"Wednesday. Indeed it is." Max danced a little jig for Noah. He couldn't help but feel a bit giddy being out and about on the forbidden day. "And here you are, sleeping the morning away!"

"But . . . but . . ."

"Noah, my friend, you've had nearly a week to get used to the idea that I'm now acquainted with the wednesdays. I really hope you'll get your ability to speak in complete sentences back soon." Max couldn't help but tease his friend. Noah just looked so ridiculous standing there in his striped pajamas with his mouth opening and closing like a fish out of water. "I told you so!" Max crowed, just to rub it in even further.

"Shhhhh!" Noah hushed him, looking around wildly. "You really have gone crazy, haven't you? You must have, to be out on a Wednesday. If my parents see you, they're likely to call the constable." Noah looked as if he still couldn't decide whether to believe Max's story.

"The constable? What's *he* going to do, arrest me? He's just as scared of the wednesdays as everyone else." Max added an extra flourish to his jig. "How about you? Want to meet them?"

Noah knew exactly who Max meant by "them." "So, they really and truly exist? You weren't lying to me?"

Max just kept dancing his silly jig.

Noah hesitated. "I don't . . . I mean, I think . . . I'm just . . ." He stopped himself and then grinned widely. "What the heck. If you can do it, then so can I. But my parents would absolutely murder me if they knew I snuck out of the house on a Wednesday, so I can't stay long."

Noah pulled on his sneakers and hoisted one leg over the windowsill. It was an easy drop down to where Max was standing, but he went no farther.

"C'mon, then." Max waved him on impatiently.

"I can't, I'm stuck on something." Noah leaned back into his room. "No worries. My shoelace just got wrapped around the radiator. I'll just give it a good tug."

It was at that moment, a split second before anything *actually* occurred, that Max knew with absolute certainty that something very bad was about to happen. "The wednesdays," he whispered, just as Noah tugged so hard on the radiator that the whole thing tore apart from his bedroom wall with a mighty creak, followed by a thunderous groan and then a loud and ominous WHOOOSHing sound.

"Ow!" Max jumped back in pain as his ankle was scalded by hot steam coming out of an air vent on the side of the house. "What the . . . ?"

"Oh, no," Noah breathed, his eyes wide. He tottered precariously above Max, with one foot in his room and the other dangling out the window. "I think that's from the boiler in the basement. I must have pulled so hard that I broke the pipes. . . ."

As if to confirm Noah's suspicion, a bloodcurdling scream sounded from an upstairs window. "Aaaah! My shower's gone ice-cold!" the voice shrieked.

"Is that Allison?" Max asked, hoping it was the slightly less screechy of Noah's two sisters.

Noah shook his head, a look of utter panic spreading across his face. "Worse. The other one."

Max heard the sound of a door opening and then another shriek, this time from a different voice. "What's going on in here? Noah?"

Max recognized the voice as belonging to Noah's mother. He dove behind a bush just in the nick of time as she rushed over to the window. "Why is this window open, Noah? Don't you realize what day it is!"

Max cowered in his hiding place as he heard Noah's father stomp into the room. "Young man, you'd better have an explanation for all of this!"

Max inched forward in the shrubbery, hoping to catch a glimpse of what was happening. Noah, still stuck halfway out the window, spotted him and waved him away frantically.

"Noah?" His mother's voice, which was shrill on a good day, was now sharp enough to cut glass. "Is there something out there?" Her voice turned panicky as she called to Noah's father. "Gunther, I think there's something out there. On a *Wednesday!*"

"I'm getting my shotgun!" Max heard the sound of Noah's father running through the house in search of his gun.

Max didn't wait around to hear more. He darted from his hiding place and ran as if his life depended on it. His life probably *did* depend on it, he realized, and then ran even faster.

He didn't stop until he reached the park, where he collapsed on a bench, nearly doubled over with a nasty cramp in his side. He had really wanted to show Noah the wednesdays, but that obviously wasn't going to happen now.

In fact, it was rapidly becoming apparent to Max that he was very much on his own as far as wednesdays were concerned.

CHAPTER 11

Sore with disappointment that Noah couldn't join him, Max decided he might as well start looking for the wednesdays in the park. It wasn't as if he had anywhere else to go. He headed toward the playground, feeling very alone and terribly sorry for himself.

Mr. Grimsrud was sitting on the park bench again. He had one shoe off and was carefully examining an impressive crop of bunions on his foot. Max approached, intending simply to say hello, but before he had even said a word, Thursday leapt from the old man's lap and growled at him ferociously.

"What has gotten into you, Thursday?" Mr. Grimsrud shrugged apologetically at Max. "He normally loves people. I've never seen him growl like that, except when he smells the wednesdays."

Max didn't feel like talking to anyone about his "condition," as his mother called it, so he simply waved and kept walking. He hoped that Thursday's growling meant the wednesdays were nearby, but it seemed more like the dog was growling at *him*. "Stupid mutt," he grumbled.

When Max didn't find any trace of the wednesdays in the park, he decided to look in the last place he had seen them—behind the grocery store. As he cut through the woods, he eyed several fallen branches and wondered if he should bring one along to use as a club, just in case things went badly. Remembering what had happened when he tried to throw the rock at one of the creatures, though, he thought better of it. *Better to just go in peacefully and get some answers*, he told himself, reluctantly leaving the large sticks behind.

Max emerged from the trees and then stopped dead in his tracks. The wednesdays were there. All of them, it seemed— clustered in one large group. They didn't look threatening, though. In fact, Max thought they looked rather friendly. Most of them had smiles on their squarish faces, and their silvery eyes sparkled cheerfully in the sunlight. One of them, who Max suspected was Ninety-eight, waved shyly.

"Next!" they called in unison in their strange, whispery voices.

"I told you, it's MAX, not Next," corrected Max, who

was beginning to suspect that perhaps their hearing wasn't very good. Why else would they keep calling him that?

The wednesdays glided out of their cluster and formed a circle around him. They all sat down on the ground except one, who was slightly larger than the rest.

"Who're you?" Max asked, wondering if he was the leader.

"*Two*," the rest of the wednesdays answered in unison for him.

"I don't mean to be rude, but why do you use numbers instead of names?" Max asked. "It seems a bit, I don't know, impersonal or something."

"*The order*," whispered all of the wednesdays except Two, who hadn't yet said anything at all.

"You're not exactly chatty, are you?" Max didn't like the way Two was silently looking at him. There was something vaguely menacing about the wednesday. "Aren't you going to say anything?"

As if in response, Two smiled broadly. It was an ugly smile pretending to be a friendly smile, though, and Max noticed with disgust that the creature's teeth were mossy green and filthy. "Welcome. We're so glad you

have joined us." The other wednesdays started giggling, until Two silenced them with a sharp hissing sound.

"I haven't joined anything," said Max crossly. "I just came to ask some questions."

For some reason this made the wednesdays clap and chant gleefully:

Questions, questions, answers none.
We talk in circles till we're done!

Max was starting to become thoroughly annoyed. "Listen, I just want to know what's happening to me. And also, why do you keep doing such nasty things to my family?"

"Who, *us?*" Two's silver eyes widened innocently. "Why, we haven't done anything at all . . . to your family."

"Birds keep pooping on my mother, my father's slippers were filled with grape jelly this morning, my baby brother's hair is *still* stained black, and all of the electrical appliances seem to be running backward, if they run at all, for starters," yelled Max. "I demand that you stop all of this, immediately!"

All of the wednesdays, including Two, laughed as if Max had said something hilarious.

Two finally quieted the group, just as Max was about to storm away. "Nex—I mean, Max. We're your friends." His voice sounded slippery and greasy, and not at all sincere. "We didn't do any of those things. *We* are not responsible." All the wednesdays looked accusingly at Max.

"You can't possibly be saying *I* did all of those things," Max protested. "That's absolutely ridiculous. Why would I do terrible things to my own family? Or to Noah, either. He's my best friend!"

The circle of wednesdays tightened, and Two looped a long, skinny, pipe-cleaner arm around Max's shoulders. "Now, now, Max. I'm not saying you *meant* to do anything unkind. But really, everyone gets upset at their parents now and then, and that cat of yours isn't exactly friendly, is he? And I don't know how you tolerate that noisy little ankle biter of a child crying at all hours. Maybe there's just a small part of you that . . . *wanted* those things to happen."

Max did not like Two's tone.

Max also did not like Two touching him—the wednesday smelled like mildew and brine.

Max could not, however, argue with what Two was saying. It was true that he didn't care much for the cat. And baby Leland really was exceptionally loud for such a small person. But Two's claim was absurd.

"No," he finally said, forcefully shoving Two's stringy arm off his shoulders. "I didn't want my mother to burn my birthday cake or get bird poop in her hair. I didn't want my dad's slippers to be ruined or his television broken. I didn't *want* any of those things to happen. And don't call Leland an ankle biter. He's a baby, and he's my brother."

"Hmmm. I suppose I *could* be mistaken." Two spoke in a sarcastic tone as he widened his silver eyes and brought one long and crooked finger to his chin.

"You most certainly *are* mistaken," Max said, glaring at the ugly creature.

Except there were a few things that Max might have kind of, sort of, *almost* thought about right before they happened—like Dr. Tetley's pants splitting or his parents' canasta cards going down the garbage disposal.

He shook his head, feeling slightly confused. "I definitely did NOT want my mother's hair to catch fire," he finally said.

Two steepled his long fingers thoughtfully. "Max," he began in his slow, slithery voice, "sometimes a . . . *naughty* thought pops into your mind—one that you can't control, right?" He didn't wait for Max to agree. "Well, your mind also has its *own* mind, and that's even naughtier."

The wednesdays were chanting again, softly this time. Max couldn't quite make out what they were saying.

"That's right." Two nodded encouragingly at the group. "So, Max, you might not *intend* to cause any harm, but your mind's mind sometimes thinks of naughty things without you even being aware. And then?" He signaled to the other wednesdays.

"*Poof!*" they screamed in unison, giggling uncontrollably. Two gestured for them to settle down, and they resumed their chanting, this time loudly enough for Max to hear:

**The mind's mind turns and the mind's
mind wheels.
Your bottom brain burns and your back
brain steals!**

Max had had quite enough. "I don't want anything bad to happen to my family, and I don't want the cat's fur to fall out! I didn't want Noah to get caught, either. I didn't do any of those things! You're all just ridiculous and awful, and I want you to leave me alone!" Max pushed his way out of the circle of wednesdays, fully prepared to fight if they tried to stop him.

They didn't try, though. They just laughed and laughed, rolling on the ground while holding their sides with their long, skinny arms and winking their glinting, silver eyes.

Max fled in disgust.

CHAPTER 12

Max didn't even try to go to sleep before midnight. Neither did his parents object to him staying up so late, since they didn't look as if they would be getting much sleep, either. They waved to him sadly through the window, and his mother blew him a kiss.

At 12:01 his father popped his head out the back door to invite him back into the house, but Max still didn't feel tired. "In a minute," he answered.

His father looked as if he wanted to say something, but he just nodded and went back inside. As he walked away, Max noticed a stoop to his shoulders and a heaviness to his footsteps that hadn't been there before. Max wanted to think his parents were so exhausted because baby Leland kept them up all hours of the night, but he had a feeling his Wednesday problems were more likely the cause.

Feeling terribly guilty, he climbed up on the roof of the house. He liked to go up there to think, and he figured that it was safe enough now, since it wasn't technically Wednesday anymore.

He lay on his back looking at the stars. From the highest point of the steep roof he could see the lights from the amusement park on the top of Mount Tibidabo. There was an airplane ride that had been Max's favorite when he was younger, and next to it an old-fashioned Ferris wheel painted in a rainbow of colors. He found it relaxing to watch the rides going around and around, and he imagined that each Ferris wheel car was filled with happy, smiling people.

Suddenly, he bolted upright. *What if it's true? What if I really am the cause of all of the bad things?* He desperately tried to recall each and every one of his thoughts from the last few minutes. Had he thought anything bad? Had he wished any harm on the people in the Ferris wheel? Had he been jealous, or spiteful, or even just thought any sort of mischievous thought, even for a moment?

He didn't *think* so, but he was filled with horror as the wheel abruptly stopped turning. He was much too far away to *actually* hear any sounds from the amusement park, but for one horrible instant he imagined he heard terrified screams coming from the people on the ride.

"No!" he cried, and shut his eyes as tightly as he could.

If he couldn't see it, then surely he couldn't hurt it. Or so he hoped. "I *don't* want anything bad to happen! I *don't* want anyone to get hurt!" He kept his eyes closed and covered his ears with his fists while he counted backward from fifty, trying to occupy his mind with the numbers and absolutely nothing else. "La, la, la," he shouted at the top of his lungs when that didn't work. His mind kept turning to the Ferris wheel, no matter how hard he tried to think of anything—*anything*—else. "Ponies and bunnies and grannies and teddies!" he yelled, over and over again.

Finally, slowly, he opened his eyes and uncovered his ears, desperately frightened that he would hear screams again—real or imagined, he was no longer sure.

The Ferris wheel was turning normally. There were no screams, nor any other sign of disaster. Everything appeared perfectly, perfectly normal.

Max sighed a huge breath of relief.

"Good thing it's not Wednesday anymore," he said out loud, vowing to control his thoughts very, very carefully in the future and to never, ever look at the Ferris wheel on a Wednesday.

Hearing his mother call him, he climbed down off the roof and went inside, finally exhausted enough to go to bed.

• • •

Max had an appointment with the out-of-town specialist on Thursday morning; the new doctor had agreed to see Max in Dr. Tetley's office for a joint consultation.

"Good morrow, madam." A strange man wearing a royal-blue cloak and bright red slippers stood up to greet them. "I daresay my reputation precedes me, but allow me to present my business card by way of introduction." With a small bow, he handed a card to Max's mother.

"Dr. Conkle-Smoak, *parapsychologist and occultist?*" his mother read incredulously from the card. "What, no fortune-tellers were available?" Her voice rose dramatically and she fixed an icy glare on Dr. Tetley. "Dr. Tetley, I need to speak to you in the hall," she hissed.

As they left the exam room Max overheard Dr. Tetley whispering to his mother, "I couldn't find anyone else, and—trust me—I called around everywhere! This isn't the sort of thing a doctor sees very often, you know." The door slammed shut.

Max picked up the card his mother had flung onto the desk:

The specialist seemed unfazed by Max's mother's reaction. He sat placidly in a faux-leather chair with his hands folded over his considerable belly. He raised one eyebrow when he caught Max looking at him. "I tune pianos, too, but that's more of a hobby," he said, gesturing to the business card.

Max decided that it would be best not to say anything until his mother returned.

When she and Dr. Tetley came back, both looked tense. "All right," Max's mother said to him quietly. "We'll give this a try. What've we got to lose?"

"Dr. Conkle-Smoak has some interesting, ah, *theories* about your case, Max," Dr. Tetley began, gesturing at the specialist to begin.

Dr. Conkle-Smoak stood to speak, as if he were lecturing to an entire classroom instead of to three very skeptical listeners. "In cases like these," he boomed, "I like to begin by placing my patients on a high-fiber diet."

"And the fiber will have a curative effect," added Dr. Tetley, nodding as if he were in complete agreement.

"No, not at all," countered Dr. Conkle-Smoak, "but I find that nearly everyone can benefit from a good bowel cleansing."

Max giggled at this, and his mother elbowed him sharply.

"Next," continued the specialist, "we need to determine the severity of the infection."

"So, it's an infection?" Max sat up hopefully. Having had numerous ear and throat infections, he knew that they could be cured with various foul-tasting remedies.

"It's an infection of sorts, but not the type you're accustomed to," answered Dr. Conkle-Smoak. "This is more like an infection of the imagination."

"I'm certainly not *imagining* the things that happen around my son on Wednesdays," objected Max's mother.

"Of course not," soothed the specialist. "That's not what I meant. But, to be truthful, I can't really be certain about anything without running some tests."

"What sort of tests?" Max eyed the strange doctor suspiciously, hoping that needles weren't involved.

Dr. Conkle-Smoak rummaged through a large satchel until he found what he was looking for. He pulled out a bulky ring and handed it to Max. "Wear this next Wednesday, and carefully make note of the colors it turns when you meet these creatures of yours. Please remember that bluish-green is different than greenish-blue. I need you to be very precise."

Max's mother yanked the ring from his hand. "This is just a mood ring," she objected. "This isn't any sort of medical test! Anyone can buy one of these at a novelty shop."

The specialist looked indignant. "Madam, it may be 'just' a mood ring, as you say, but not everyone is an expert in diagnosing the results. I spent seven years studying the science of psychic chromatography, and in my skilled hands this ring is a precise diagnostic tool."

His mother rolled her eyes. "He's as sharp as a donut, this one," she said, a bit meanly. But the doctor didn't seem to take offense. After giving the matter a moment of thought, she stood up and handed the ring back to Max with a shrug of defeat. "What've we got to lose," she repeated to herself sadly as they walked out of the office.

CHAPTER 13

Max's mother let him skip the rest of the school day on Thursday, and then again on Friday. She didn't say it in so many words, but Max strongly suspected that she let him stay home because baby Leland had developed a strange, new fascination with him. Prior to Max's run-in with the wednesdays, Leland had cried and fussed louder than ever when Max tried to play with him. He simply wasn't a playing kind of baby. Instead he was a yowling, fussing, spitting-up kind of baby, and in Max's opinion, not very fun to be around.

Now, however, baby Leland immediately stopped his fussing the instant Max entered the room. Occasionally, he even went as far as holding out his arms and cooing at Max to lift him.

"See?" said their mother. "I told you that he would eventually outgrow his colic and want to play with his big brother!"

And with that, she lay down on the sofa and promptly fell asleep, having spent the previous seven months up at all hours with the baby.

But, as much as Max *wanted* to be a good older brother, he had a sneaking suspicion that baby Leland's new fascination with him had more to do with the wednesdays than anything else. He couldn't be certain, of course, but Leland seemed strangely preoccupied with staring into Max's eyes, almost as if he could see his reflection in them. It was slightly flattering—and slightly creepy.

Then, because it rained heavily all weekend long, Max ended up spending Saturday and Sunday indoors, watching old movies on the TV that his father had finally managed to repair and dodging requests from his parents to join them in a game of canasta. He called Noah once, but the conversation had been a short one.

"I'm telling Mom! You're not supposed to be on the phone, you little weasel!" Max could hear Noah's sister shrieking in the background. "Get off!"

"I can't talk now," Noah said breathlessly. "I'm grounded this weekend. See you Monday?" The sound of a vigorous wrestling match for control over the phone ended with an abrupt click, followed by a dial tone.

Max hung up glumly, hoping Noah wasn't too angry with him.

• • •

By Monday morning he was more than ready to get out of the house and go back to school. Four days of dodging baby Leland's spit-up projectiles was quite enough. Besides, he hadn't seen Noah since their ill-fated encounter on the previous Wednesday, and he was anxious to see how his friend had fared.

He still hadn't decided whether to tell anyone else about the wednesdays, but as he walked up the steps of the school-house Monday morning, he concluded that it would be better to wait until he had some sort of proof.

As it turned out, he didn't have to tell anyone at all. The entire school had already heard.

• • •

When Max entered the crowded, noisy hallway, everyone immediately stopped talking. Groups of students parted as he walked by, everyone stepping hurriedly out of his path. At one point, a particularly high-strung fifth grader backed into Max as he walked by and literally jumped into the air with a high-pitched squeal when he saw who he had bumped against.

Max was puzzled at first. Then he saw Peter Tetley leaning smugly against a drinking fountain.

Peter Tetley was Dr. Tetley's son.

Peter Tetley had hated Max with a burning passion ever since the third grade, when Max had sort-of-accidentally (but kind-of-on-purpose) told a few of their classmates that Peter had wet the bed at a sleepover. It had been years now, but Peter had finally found his chance for revenge.

It immediately became clear that Peter had gleefully told the entire school about Max's case of the wednesdays, no doubt embellishing the story along the way.

Max groaned and hurried to the refuge of his locker. Where the heck was Noah? Max knew that his best friend was chronically tardy, but he'd hoped Noah would show up on time just this once.

He was pretending to concentrate on opening the combination lock when Max sensed someone approach him. He whirled around defensively, but it was only Gemma Swift. Not that there was anything "only" about Gemma, who carried out her role as the editor of the school's newspaper with an intensity Max had always found both puzzling and more than a little intimidating. Her usual cluster of student reporters stood nearby, giggling nervously.

"Max," Gemma began confidently, as if she were conducting a professional interview. "We"—she gestured back to her twittering friends—"heard a little rumor about you."

Max held his breath while he considered whether he should simply deny everything.

Gemma leaned in closer. "Is it true that you actually met

them? The . . . *wednesdays?*" She whispered the word as if it were dangerous to even say aloud.

Max suddenly realized that he could use his story to his advantage. After all, he was the only person who had ever *met* the creatures. He could be a local celebrity!

But just then, Peter chimed in and ruined everything.

"I wouldn't get too close to him," Peter yelled louder than necessary from across the hall. "My father says that he could be contagious."

Gemma took a step back toward the safety of her giggling group, but she kept her eye contact with Max. "What are they like?" She hushed her friends with a hand gesture. Several other girls, emboldened by Gemma's presence, drew nearer to listen.

"Well," said Max. "Since you asked—"

"Honestly, everyone. Keep your distance," Peter interrupted rudely. "My father is talking to the school principal right now because he thinks Max is a health threat. He shouldn't be allowed in public places."

Gemma looked skeptical, but she took another step back. So did all of the other girls.

Max glared at Peter. What right did he have to tell everyone? Max opened his mouth, about to shout an angry insult, when the drinking fountain suddenly turned on, dousing the front of Peter's pants.

Max laughed and pointed tauntingly. "Have a little accident, did we, Peter?"

But no one else was laughing.

"Oh my goodness," Gemma breathed. "Where's my photographer? Did anyone get a picture of that?"

The circle around Max widened as all of the students shrank away from him.

"It's true!" Peter shouted. "He's a menace. He's a . . . *wednesday*. You all just saw what he did. I'm going to tell my father and the principal." He turned and stalked wetly down the hall as the school bell rang.

Max hurried to his classroom and scrunched down in his assigned seat as far as he could. He was utterly confused. He had been furious with Peter, it was true, but he hadn't intentionally made the water fountain spray him. But when it happened, it was as if it had just . . . felt right. And he *might* have been thinking about Peter's bed-wetting incident somewhere in the back of his mind. Perhaps there really was something to Two's idea of his mind's mind making bad things happen.

"But today is Monday," Max said out loud, puzzled. Regina Olsen, who normally sat in the desk next to Max's, leapt from her seat and moved hurriedly to the back of the classroom, a panicky look on her face.

Only then did Max realize that *all* of the desks around

his were empty. The students who usually sat near him were instead standing clustered in worried groups at the front of the room. He looked around one more time for Noah, who was still missing in action. At least his best friend would stand by him—if he ever showed up, that is.

"Oh, come on, everyone," he protested. "I'm not dangerous!"

No one responded. No one would even look him in the eye.

The classroom door opened and Mrs. Trimersnide, the teacher, walked in with Mr. Alderwood, the school principal. Max was grateful for the distraction until Mr. Alderwood pointed directly at him and then beckoned for Max to follow him out into the hall.

Max's stomach sank. He suspected that his day was about to get even worse.

CHAPTER 14

"**S**uspended?"

Max knew the look on his mother's face—it was the same look she'd had when she threatened to throw a large rock at Dr. Tetley's cracked window.

"Now, Mrs. Bernard, please calm down. We have to consider the safety of *all* of the students, and we've never had a . . . *situation* quite like this before. We need to exercise an abundance of caution." Mr. Alderwood pushed nervously on his glasses and dabbed at his brow with a handkerchief.

"You call this an 'abundance of caution'?" His mother's voice rose even further. "I call this an abundance of—"

Max's father cut her off quickly. "Dear, let's not get overly excited here. I'm sure we can talk this over and come to a nice compromise." He was bouncing baby Leland on his lap, although he needn't have bothered. The baby was utterly transfixed by Max, staring at him as though hypnotized.

Mr. Alderwood fidgeted and dabbed again at his damp face. "Well, sir," he began nervously, "I'm afraid we really can't continue this discussion here. Dr. Tetley has advised the school board that Max's presence puts the entire educational community at risk." His voice quavered as Max's mother's mouth started to open and her fists began to clench. "So I have no choice but to ask you to leave the premises."

The principal was sweating profusely by now, and Max realized that Mr. Alderwood had pushed his chair as far away from him as the small office allowed. "I'd be happy to schedule a telephone conference to discuss the matter further, of course. Say, same time next week?" He ducked as both of Max's parents jumped angrily to their feet. Baby Leland's trance was broken by the sudden movement, and he started to cry.

Max couldn't believe what was happening. "You're all treating me like a . . . like some sort of a *leper*," he cried out. He didn't mind the suspension so much, but he was genuinely hurt by the way the other students had treated him. They were *supposed* to be his friends!

"You'll be hearing from our lawyer," his mother announced firmly as she snatched up baby Leland and then pulled both Max and his father from the office.

"Dear, we don't even *have* a lawyer," his father whispered as they left the school building.

His mother waved this comment away and then sniffled into a tissue.

Max felt rotten; it was the worst day of his life so far, and it wasn't even ten o'clock in the morning yet.

● ● ●

They walked the rest of the way in a tense silence that was broken only by the occasional surly howl from baby Leland. When they got home, Max's father went out to work in the garden, and his mother went in to prepare lunch. Max retreated to his tree house. He needed to do some serious thinking.

CHAPTER 15

Max sat cross-legged in his tree house, replaying the morning's events in his mind. He was particularly troubled by the drinking fountain incident. *How could that happen on a Monday?* He had thought his "infection," as Dr. Conkle-Smoak called it, only showed up on Wednesdays. That was what made it "a case of the wednesdays," after all.

But Max knew deep down that he had caused the water fountain to spray Peter. He also knew this could only mean one thing: he was getting worse.

A terrifying thought occurred to him, and he scrambled down the tree house ladder as his fear began to grow. He raced into the house, ran past his stunned mother, and headed directly for the bathroom mirror. He studied his reflection intently for several minutes, but he couldn't make up his mind. Did his eyes look slightly silvery, or didn't they?

There seemed to be a bit of an extra sparkle, but it wasn't quite enough for him to tell if they had changed or not. Baby Leland sure seemed fascinated by his eyes lately, though, which Max took as a bad sign. Did his little brother see something that he couldn't?

He walked out of the bathroom so lost in thought that he stubbed his toe on the leg of the sofa before he even realized he had wandered into the living room.

"Maxwell," his mother called to him from where she sat on the floor, playing with baby Leland. "Look at you! Your clothes hardly fit you at all—your trousers look awfully tight in the tummy, and your shirtsleeves are way too short. If you can't be in school today, we might as well take you shopping. The other mothers in the village already think I'm the worst parent around, and I won't have them see you walking about in ill-fitting clothes."

Max gasped and ran back toward the bathroom. "What did I say?" his mother asked, baffled.

Max slammed the door behind him, feeling faint. He kept his back to the mirror for a moment, afraid to look. Slowly, carefully, he turned around to study his reflection again in the full-length mirror mounted on the back of the door. He felt the blood drain from his face as he realized that his mother was right—the waistband of his pants *was* too tight on him. His wrists poked out of his long sleeves farther than they should, too, whereas his pant legs were puddling around his ankles. A feeling of horror nearly overcame him as he twisted and turned to look at his reflection from different angles. There was no denying it: his arms were starting to look stretched out and gangly, while his torso and legs were becoming squatter and rounder . . . *just like the wednesdays*. He peered cautiously into the mirror again. He couldn't be entirely certain, but his neck did seem slightly shorter than it had just the day before.

He sat down on the bathroom floor, stunned. If his suspicions were true, then he didn't just have a case of the wednesdays. It was much, much worse than that.

If his suspicions were true, he was *becoming* one.

●　●　●

Max's father was outside watering the lawn when Max rushed out of the house. "Whoa, there, son," he called out. "What's your hurry?"

"Sorry, Dad. I'll be back soon." Max scooted past with an apologetic wave. He didn't have time to chat. He was in search of answers.

He looked for the wednesdays in all the places he had seen them before, but he didn't find any sign of them, naturally. It was only Monday. He was going to have to wait two whole days before he could confront the creatures to demand some answers.

The village was quiet—not as deserted as it was on Wednesdays, of course, but hardly anyone was out and about. Max was grateful for the privacy—he had an experiment to conduct, and he didn't want anyone watching.

He spent several minutes deciding on a target. He wished that he understood more about what the mind's mind was, and what it was capable of doing. But perhaps he could find out on his own. He spotted a trash can and got to work.

Max sat on a bench and focused all of his thoughts on the trash can. He concentrated as hard as he could manage, struggling to push through the worries and distractions. *Focus.* He took a deep breath, and then tried to mentally picture the can tipping over and spilling.

Nothing happened.

He tried to imagine a stiff breeze whisking away the discarded paper that was piled to the brim.

Nothing happened.

He tried to use his mind to bend the soda can sticking out of the mound of trash. He started to get a headache from squinting so hard, but nothing else happened.

He sat back on the bench and exhaled loudly. Was it

possible that the water fountain incident was just a bizarre coincidence? Maybe there was nothing wrong with him after all.

Max was fidgeting on the bench, trying to get more comfortable so that he could try again, when a man wearing an obvious toupee strolled by and then sat down on a nearby bench. He unfolded a newspaper, crinkling and rustling it far more than was actually necessary, and then began to read. He whistled tunelessly as he paged through the sports section.

Max tried to ignore the man—he had enough on his mind already—but the whistling seemed to invade his every thought. Generally speaking, Max didn't object to whistling, but for some reason this particular whistle was grating on his nerves. The noise just seemed awfully shrill and excessively loud, and the man wasn't even bothering to follow any kind of pattern or song. The high-pitched noise droned on and on; it hardly seemed as if the man even needed to ever take a breath, his whistling was just so blasted constant. Max grimaced and put his hands over his ears, trying to block out the horrible, horrible sound. The thought occurred to him that he might go truly insane if he had to sit and listen to that terrible noise for another second.

The truth of the matter was that Max had had a very bad day, and he was in a very foul mood. The annoying whistler was the final straw, and the shrill noise became the focus of every speck of irritation, anger, and hostility that Max was feeling. Max couldn't control much of what was happening in his life, but how he wanted that maddening, tuneless noise to stop! He was about to yell at the man to knock it off when the man's furry hairpiece abruptly flew straight up in the air and then began to float toward the park entrance, carried by a sudden, stiff breeze. The man jumped up from his seat to grab the toupee, but his shoelaces had become tangled, and he nearly tripped. He recovered his balance just in time to keep from falling over, but he had to hobble awkwardly after his hairpiece until one of the shoelaces finally broke, allowing him to sprint after his disappearing wig.

Problem solved was the first thought that popped into Max's head. It was followed quickly, however, by the realization that he had much bigger problems than an annoying whistler.

He had obviously caused the man's toupee to fly away.

Max clapped his hands over his mouth, then changed his mind and covered his eyes instead. What was the use, though? He couldn't block his thoughts by covering any part of his face. No, his face wasn't the problem at all. *How do you block a brain?* he wondered.

He hadn't been thinking anything about the man's

hairpiece in particular—he hadn't planned anything quite so specific as that. But all of his thoughts *had* been focused on just how annoyed he was feeling, and just how much he had wanted the whistling to stop.

"The mind's mind . . . ," Max whispered to himself as he started to realize just how complicated his problem really was. It seemed that he couldn't choose precisely what to do with his new powers, but some part of his mind was obviously making the decisions for him. He tried to remember what the wednesdays had called it . . . the bottom brain? Max wondered if there was some way to learn to have more control over the power. He didn't like it when birds pooped on his mom or when his dad's television broke, but he did quite like the idea of being able to mess with people like Peter Tetley.

Having a case of the wednesdays might not be *all* terrible, he realized—especially if he could learn to control his mind's mind. For the first time in days he suddenly felt ravenous, so he headed home for lunch.

CHAPTER 16

Max didn't have any more incidents over the next two days. But staying at home all day was mind-numbingly dull, and when he woke up on Wednesday morning, he realized that he was actually looking forward to seeing what the day would bring. That is, he was looking forward to it until, halfway through his morning shower, he discovered that his shampoo bottle had been filled with motor oil. "Argh," he groaned as he fumbled, soaking wet, through the bathroom cabinet in search of actual *soap* to clean his dripping, greasy scalp. "Why do they always have to mess with the hair?"

It was definitely Wednesday.

He ate his breakfast hurriedly and then gave his mother a quick kiss on the cheek. "Sorry again about your bathrobe."

"It's all right, dear. I'm sure the stain will come out." She smoothed her hand over the new ink spots on her white robe. Neither of them mentioned the incident involving the cat and the vacuum cleaner earlier that morning; Max sincerely hoped that both would be okay.

"Be *very* careful out there." Max's mother looked worried, but she didn't bother to try to stop him from going out. Baby Leland had just slept through the entire night for the first time ever in his short life, and Max's parents were both looking positively blissful from the unaccustomed rest. And although they didn't speak it, Max could sense the question lingering in the air: could it have something to do with the wednesdays?

As he trudged down the front steps and headed toward the deserted village center, this unspoken question turned darker in his mind. His well-rested parents almost seemed to be turning him over willingly—sacrificing him, even—to the wednesdays in return for a less-colicky baby Leland and a full night's sleep.

No, that's nonsense, he told himself. It was *his* idea to go out on a Wednesday, after all. He shook off the thought and picked up his pace. But even as he raced off, eagerly and of his own accord, the unpleasant idea had left behind its tender bruise deep within Max's thoughts.

• • •

He didn't find any sign of the wednesdays in the park or behind the grocery store. Every few minutes he glanced down at the heavy mood ring Dr. Conkle-Smoak had given him. So far it hadn't done much more than change from grayish-purple to grayish-purplish-yellow, but Max was mindful of the specialist's instruction to keep careful track of the colors.

He finally stumbled across Ninety-eight and two other wednesdays outside the village's small movie theater. They were staring intently at the marquee. Max looked up and saw that the letters on the sign had been rearranged to spell something *very* naughty.

"That's not very nice," he chastised the wednesdays. "Now someone is going to have to climb up a ladder to fix it."

"We didn't do it," they chimed in unison.

"Yeah, yeah, the mind's mind and all that—I know. Look, you all need to start taking some responsibility," Max lectured them sternly. "I'm certain you could stop doing all these mean things if you tried."

The wednesdays just giggled stupidly, as usual. Max was starting to wonder if they weren't a bit simpleminded.

"Wednesdays aren't for responsibility," Ninety-eight said very seriously, as if he were quoting someone wiser than himself. "There are plenty of other days for *that*."

Max groaned—they were truly hopeless. "Who're you?"

he asked Ninety-eight's companions. It dawned on him that he was starting to be able to tell the wednesdays apart. At first he had thought they all looked mostly the same, but now he could see that they were, in fact, each as unique as any regular person.

"Sixty-one," answered one of the wednesdays, who was very small and had a higher and younger-sounding voice than the others.

"Sixty-two," said the second, who was broad-shouldered and tall, but otherwise bore a strong resemblance to Sixty-one.

Max was just about to ask what it meant that their names were so close together when the smaller one told him without being asked. "We was brothers. Before, I mean."

"What do you mean, you *were* brothers? Aren't you brothers now?"

All three wednesdays looked vaguely puzzled by this question, as if they had never before even considered the possibility.

"It's just different now," Sixty-two finally answered, shrugging. "That's Ninety-nine over there. He's the newest one." He gestured behind them. Max hadn't even noticed there was another wednesday present; Ninety-nine was cowering in a corner, and his silver eyes were wide with fright. He didn't speak or even acknowledge the others.

Max remembered that he was supposed to be keeping

track of the mood ring colors. He looked down and was surprised to see that although the stone was still mostly grayish, there were now also several bright yellow stripes rippling across the surface.

"Ooh, pretty," admired Ninety-eight, who was looking at the ring so covetously that Max felt compelled to let him try it on.

Ninety-eight danced and shrieked happily as he tried on the mood ring. It was way too big for his long, skinny finger, but the ring began to change color anyway as soon as Ninety-eight took it in his hand. Max and the others leaned in and watched as bright colors began to swirl around the ring's surface in a constantly changing rainbow pattern.

"I didn't know mood rings could do that," whispered Max, who wished that Dr. Conkle-Smoak was there to interpret the colors for him.

"Ooooh," admired the two other wednesdays.

Ninety-eight gawked at the ring for several minutes before passing it to the brothers. The ring continued to change colors when both Sixty-one and Sixty-two wore it; on their fingers the colors were even brighter, and the patterns even more dramatic.

A thought began to grow in Max's head as he watched the wednesdays playing with the ring. "You really like that ring, don't you?" he asked slyly.

The wednesdays nodded, but they were so entranced by the ring that they hardly seemed to hear him.

"Maybe I could let you keep the ring for a little while. . . ." He smiled as the wednesdays' silver eyes widened hopefully. "In exchange for some information, that is."

The three wednesdays eagerly agreed, and then began to wrestle for control over the ring. "Me first," shouted Sixty-two, holding it out of Sixty-one's reach.

Max let them bicker over the ring for a few minutes while he considered what to ask them. He figured it was better to ask them questions while they were distracted anyway, so that they didn't get suspicious.

He started with the basics. "Who is in charge?"

"Oldest first, number One," answered Sixty-one in a singsong voice.

Sixty-two gave his little brother an abrupt shove. "No. Two is in charge—I told you that. Don't let him hear you talking about One."

"Wait, so your names are in order?" Max was starting to understand. "But then One would be older than Two. Shouldn't he be the leader?"

None of the wednesdays seemed to want to answer. "We don't talk about One anymore," Ninety-eight finally answered.

"You'll be One!" The squeaky voice came from several

feet away. Max had completely forgotten about Ninety-nine, who was still hiding in the corner.

Ninety-eight shushed him dismissively. "One-*Hundred*. That's different."

"Two doesn't think so," said the squeaky voice in the corner.

Max was struggling to understand. He didn't *want* to understand. "You mean . . . I'm next," he finally whispered. "I'm going to be a wednesday?"

The other wednesdays had become distracted by the ring again, though, and no one answered him. They were tossing it back and forth, squealing each time the color shifted. Soon they started chanting as they tossed the ring:

Chaos, mayhem, plain bad luck.
One day a week we run amok.
Making trouble is what we do.
In a week of Wednesdays, so will you!

Even Ninety-nine joined in the chanting. After a few minutes Max couldn't take it anymore. "Stop!" he shouted. "What do you mean, a week of Wednesdays?"

Ninety-eight giggled. "In seven Wednesdays, silly. Then you'll be one of us. You'll be One Hundred." He continued to toss the ring with the others, oblivious to Max's panicked reaction.

Max broke into a clammy sweat. On a hunch, he asked a question that he didn't entirely want to hear the answer to. "Where did you all come from?" It came out in a whisper.

"Here and there. Everywhere!" Sixty-one answered in a singsong voice, and Max wondered if he was confused by the question. But the others soon joined in with him, skipping rhythmically to their latest chant:

One from here,
One from there.
Wednesdays come from everywhere.
There to here,
Once a year.
Once a year of Wednesdays!

"Except me," Sixty-two interrupted with a sulky expression on his face. "I wasn't supposed to come."

"He wouldn't let go when the week ended," Sixty-one added in his babyish voice, as if that explained anything at all.

The possibility that these . . . these *creatures* might have once been boys just like himself filled Max with a sense of horror. While the others continued their dancing and chanting, Ninety-eight leaned in toward him. In a quiet, conspiratorial tone, the wednesday began to speak. "Watch out for Two. He's planning to—"

Ninety-eight broke off suddenly as an impossibly long arm appeared from out of nowhere and a hand that looked like an animal's claw snatched the ring out of midair. The other wednesdays abruptly stopped their chanting and cowered in fear as Two slowly fit the ring onto one of his long, snakelike fingers.

"That'll be enough out of *you*," Two hissed at Ninety-eight, who whimpered slightly.

Max's eyes widened as he watched the ring turn a dull black with a crimson dot surrounded by a poisonous-looking green band in the center.

Max didn't need Dr. Conkle-Smoak's help to interpret the ring. If evil had a color, then this was it.

CHAPTER 17

"Maxwell," Two purred insincerely. A smell of mold and decay wafted from his body, and his teeth seemed to have added yet another layer of moss.

Max glared at the wednesday. Only his mother called him Maxwell.

"It's only natural that you have questions. But *they* don't know anything." Two waved dismissively at the others.

Sixty-one looked like he was about to cry, and Ninety-nine had vanished completely.

"Come. Join us at Council," invited Two smoothly. "You'll learn more than you ever wanted to know."

The other wednesdays, who were already pale to begin with, turned a shade even lighter with the mention of the word *Council*.

Max, on the other hand, welcomed the chance to finally get some answers. "Lead the way," he dared.

Two's face twisted into a sneer and Max realized that he must be learning to tell the difference between the various wednesdays. He now saw that Two was easily distinguishable from the others. His eyes were a duller silver, more of a gunmetal gray, really—and they gave his expression a cold, cruel edge. Two's mossy teeth looked longer and pointier than Max remembered from the previous week, too. He definitely looked . . . *meaner* than the other wednesdays.

Max followed as Two glided toward the Council. Sixty-two had to tug on Sixty-one's hand to persuade him to follow, and Ninety-eight shuffled reluctantly behind them.

Two led the motley group toward the school and then into the gymnasium. Max wasn't at all surprised to see that the lock on the door had been broken. The room looked as if there had been quite a wednesday party inside: streamers and torn paper were littered about, and the floor was covered in a sticky liquid. Two clambered underneath the bleachers and then disappeared. Max had to search for a moment before he spotted the opening. There was no door, but a makeshift entrance had been created by cutting a ragged, gaping hole in the wall. It looked like the world's largest rat had chewed its way through the plaster and wood.

He was barely able to squeeze through the hole—he was still taller than most of the wednesdays, after all, at least for the moment. He'd had to roll his pants up when he dressed that morning, though, so his height advantage might not be for long. Strands of cobwebs and several actual spiders clung to his hair and clothing by the time he made it through the hole. He brushed himself off with disgust and looked around. They were in some sort of large storage room that had obviously been long since forgotten by school officials. The room was in a state of utter chaos—broken desks were stacked like kindling, mildewed textbooks were scattered everywhere, and the walls were lined with dusty shelves containing everything from crusty tubs of long-dried paste to broken sticks of chalk.

Most of the wednesdays were already in the room, and their wrestling and dancing about had stirred up great clouds of dust. Max sneezed, and then rolled his eyes in exasperation when several of the wednesdays imitated him.

Two brought the meeting to order by running his claw-like fingernails down an old chalkboard. The horrible sound made Max cover his ears, but it didn't seem to faze anyone else. Several of the wednesdays continued to frolic noisily in the corner. Two narrowed his gray eyes at them, and they were suddenly flung violently to the ground. One of the wednesdays whimpered slightly and slunk away, but otherwise the room grew silent.

"Welcome to Council, my fellow wednesdays. It's been *far* too long." Two was grinning his brutish, malevolent grin again. He was the only one smiling. None of the other wednesdays looked particularly happy to be there.

"We'll start with the good news—the first item on our agenda is Awards and Recognition. Let's all give a hand to Six, who not only let all of the cows escape from the dairy barn, but also managed to curdle every last bit of the cream in the storage tank."

This cheered the group slightly. They stomped and hissed happily as Two hung what looked like a garland made out of yarn and rusty metal springs around Six's neck.

Two rattled off several more awards, including Most Tires Flattened, Best Use of Glue, and an honorable mention for Most Loud Screams.

Max noticed that each of the award recipients had a name lower than Ten. The older wednesdays appeared to be hairier and broader than the rest of the group. They still had the same stringy, bendy arms and short, squat torsos and legs as the younger wednesdays, but their fingernails were longer, their eyes narrower, and they were just plain *uglier*. Max wondered if they got smellier as they aged, too, when one of the award recipients brushed by him and he got a powerful whiff of what smelled like a combination of cheese gone bad, public restroom, and unwashed feet.

By the time Two finished handing out awards, he was surrounded by all of the most senior wednesdays. In the dim light of the storage room they looked like a jury of ghouls. Two was still wearing the mood ring, and even in the cobweb-darkened room, the center of the stone glowed blood red.

The other wednesdays still seemed to be having a good time with the awards ceremony, though. Several of the smaller wednesdays had formed an impromptu cheerleading squad. Using ancient, stained mopheads as pom-poms, they chanted enthusiastically as each winner was announced:

Hooray for messes!
Bravo for screams!
If it distresses,
It's from one of our team!

The wednesdays stomped their feet and clapped for each award. Their stomping stirred up so much dust that Max's eyes started to water in protest. Some of the cheerleaders attempted to form a pyramid, but after teetering briefly in a formation three wednesdays high, they collapsed in a heap, creating a huge dust cloud.

Perhaps because there was so much dust in the air, Max didn't notice any sort of signal, but suddenly the mood of the room changed. A hush fell over the wednesdays, and they silently began arranging themselves into neat rows by order of name.

The wednesdays were usually a giggling, fidgeting group, but now they stood at crisp attention. The group started to chant again, but now their chant lacked any of the singsong happiness of their earlier rhymes. This time they sounded robotic and cheerless:

We are in order.
We are in rows.
The Council can start,
And anything goes.

The sudden shift gave Max chills. He shivered, wishing he hadn't agreed to come to Council after all.

Two began to speak in a low, authoritarian tone. "The wednesday Tribunal"—he gestured at the oldest and the ugliest wednesdays, who stood tightly clustered behind him— "has met. We have some very serious infractions to address." His face broke into his menacing, toothy sneer. "And I will warn you now that the punishments will be *severe*."

CHAPTER 18

Two read the charges while Three, a hunchbacked wednesday with a gruesome scar crisscrossing his face, acted as a bailiff, yanking the offenders out of their rows to stand in judgment.

"Reckless Goodwill."

Three shoved one of the wednesdays to the front of the room for this charge, while the rest of the group stood stiffly, their silver eyes cast downward.

"Failure to Destroy."

The accused wednesday started to protest, but he stopped immediately when Three bared his teeth and growled threateningly.

"Orderly Conduct, and an additional charge of Absence of Malice."

A wide-eyed Ninety-eight was pulled from the crowd.

"And, finally, this individual is charged with one count of each of the following crimes: Neglect of Negligence, Mutiny Against Bedlam, and Gross Disregard for Pandemonium."

The other wednesdays gasped at the severity of the charges as Ninety-nine was dragged roughly from his hiding place in the darkest corner of the room. He was mute with terror.

Max felt sorry for the youngest wednesday, who was visibly trembling. He simply couldn't just sit back and watch. "Those are absolutely ridiculous charges," he called out loudly, stepping forward. "None of those things are even real crimes."

Even as the words left his mouth, he knew that it would probably be wiser to stay out of the wednesdays' affairs, but he didn't like the way the older creatures bullied the younger, smaller ones. It simply wasn't right.

"My, my. Aren't you a cheeky young human." Far from becoming angry, though, Two smiled slyly at Max's outburst—almost as if he had been waiting for it. "If you object to our charges, then you are certain to find our punishments even worse." Two snapped with his long, spidery fingers at Three, who lumbered over to the first of the accused wednesdays.

The smaller creature tried to run away, but Three, whose arms seemed freakishly long, even by wednesday standards, grabbed him roughly by the spot on his body that would have been a throat, if he'd had more of a neck.

As Three held the whimpering wednesday up by his nearly nonexistent neck, Two announced his verdict. "We find you guilty as charged."

He paused as the rest of the wednesdays solemnly chanted "*guilty*" in their eerie, trancelike chorus.

Two continued cheerfully. "I hereby sentence you to tipping over forty full garbage cans, stealing fifteen completed homework assignments, and jamming the locks of three dozen doors."

"But that will take forever," the convicted wednesday protested in a squeaky, strangled voice.

"Nonsense. It's just a matter of hard work and dedication." Two dismissed him with a wave of the hand.

Max *had* to say something. "You're deranged. You're telling him to do things that are just horrible!" He turned to the other wednesdays in the rows. "Why do you all listen to him? He's positively savage. There's no need for you to be so destructive. There's no call for *any* of this Tribunal nonsense!" But none of the other wednesdays responded. They remained silent, staring down at their feet.

Once again, it seemed that Two had been anticipating Max's actions. Two widened his flinty eyes in mock innocence and spoke in a taunting tone. "Well, then, Max, perhaps you might prefer to come up with the rest of the sentences yourself." He gestured toward the remaining three wednesday convicts.

Max knew that this was some kind of trick. It had to be. But he couldn't tell what Two was up to.

Watching Max struggle to make sense of everything, Two made a further offer. "For every sentence you impose, we will respond to one question. I *know* that you have lots of questions, don't you?"

That clinched it. Knowing full well that Two was up to no good, Max nodded his agreement. He needed information, even if this *was* a trick.

Without being told, the wednesdays broke their ranks and formed a large circle with Max in the center. Max tried to read their expressions, but none of the creatures would meet his eyes.

"Will the accused step forward," demanded Two. Three didn't wait for anyone to step forward, though—he grabbed the small wednesday by the arm and flung him into the center of the circle.

"Max, this wednesday has been found guilty of the crime of Failure to Destroy. He was seen walking by a rose garden without so much as wilting a single flower or uprooting a single bush. This is clearly unacceptable." Two prompted the others by raising an eyebrow.

"*Guilty*," the other wednesdays chanted in unison.

"And now, dear Max, your job is to assign a fitting punishment." Two's voice lowered into a threatening growl: "Or else *we* will." The senior Tribunal members all bared their teeth and hissed like wild animals.

Max turned to face the convicted wednesday, who cowered before him. He winked at the small creature to reassure him that nothing bad would happen.

And then he realized that he had absolutely *no* idea what to do next.

First he tried to think of a punishment. On more than one occasion during his life in the village Max had been the victim of what the locals called a "wednesday pants-ing." This involved having your trousers suddenly fall to your ankles, usually while you were walking or running, which caused the victim to stumble and fall. This common occurrence alone was embarrassing enough to keep many villagers from venturing out of the safety—and *privacy*—of their homes on Wednesdays. It seemed like a suitable punishment to Max, and he had enough experience with it that he thought he might be able to make it happen.

But, just as he couldn't use his new powers in the park when he tried to focus on the trash can, neither could he drop the wednesday's trousers, no matter how hard he concentrated.

He tried with his eyes open. He tried with his eyes closed. Nothing happened.

Two tapped his toe loudly and impatiently. "Just let me

know if you need me to take over," he offered, not at all kindly.

Max ignored him and decided to try a different approach. Remembering what had happened earlier in the park, he stopped trying to focus on a particular outcome. Instead, he closed his eyes and thought about just how much he was starting to dislike Two. *He doesn't think that I can do it. But if I can just make something happen, then he'll have to answer a question. I'll show that detestable monster. . . .* Max was thinking so intently that he didn't even realize anything had happened until he heard a loud racket, accompanied by surprised gasps from the wednesdays in the room.

CHAPTER 19

Max opened his eyes just in time to see an avalanche of sports equipment burying the wednesday standing in front of him.

A deluge of soccer balls, basketballs, and half-deflated red rubber balls rained down onto the unfortunate wednesday. Max winced as he watched a hard baseball bounce off the top of the creature's head. One of the storage shelves had broken, and the contents—the ghosts of sports teams past—were spilling out all over the stunned wednesday.

Max vaguely realized that the balls seemed to be falling . . . *farther* than they should have. He was no physics expert, but it looked like the balls were going out of their way to hit the convicted wednesday, while missing everyone else.

Just when it seemed that the avalanche of balls had

stopped, a carton of golf balls rolled off the broken shelf and ricocheted musically off the wednesday's forehead—*tok tok tok tok tok!*

The room was completely silent for a moment. Then the punished wednesday, still surrounded by balls from every sport, raised his silver gaze to look into Max's bewildered face. Slowly, his face broke into a smile, and he grinned broadly at his punisher. The rest of the wednesdays began to shriek with giggles, and even Max chuckled a bit, although he felt very confused.

Two clapped his clawed hands slowly and sarcastically. "Not bad, Max. Not bad at all for your first Council. A bit lenient, perhaps, but it's a decent start. Now, let's move on to the next—"

"Wait," Max interrupted. "I get to ask a question now."

Two frowned peevishly, but he waggled his fingers at Max to proceed.

All the silver eyes in the room turned toward Max. The wednesdays leaned forward, waiting to hear what his question would be. Max opened his mouth to ask his question, only to realize he had *no* idea what to ask. He had a million questions, of course, but where should he start? He wanted to know a little bit about everything, but he couldn't quite come up with the right way to ask anything at all. He bit his tongue nervously, annoyed at himself for not planning better. Different topics raced wildly through his head. The dust in the room, the dim lighting provided by the two bare lightbulbs, the rank smell of the wednesdays, and the truly disturbing way that Three was glowering at him were all starting to make him feel a bit dizzy. A droplet of sweat trickled down the side of his face.

"Perhaps another time," Two started to say, and Max knew that he had to ask *something* or else lose his chance forever.

So, with a thousand thoughts competing to come out, he opened his mouth again and asked the first thing that popped into his head. "Why aren't there any girl wednesdays?"

Stupid, stupid, stupid! He berated himself silently the moment the words left his lips. Of all the questions he really *needed* to ask, why did this pointless question pop out? He raked his fingers through his sweaty hair in frustration, certain he had wasted his opportunity.

Max's question caused quite a stir among the wednesdays, though. The younger creatures twittered, the older ones gasped, and Two's brow creased in anger. Then Max realized that Two wasn't *angry*—he was *embarrassed!* Swirly pink blotches bloomed on his pale face until he looked like a strawberry sundae. His mouth opened and closed wordlessly, like he either couldn't or didn't want to answer the question.

Two, Max realized, was absolutely, completely mortified.

At their own peril, the other wednesdays answered for him. In fact, they seemed positively eager to answer.

"Silly," squeaked one of the creatures, in a strange, high-pitched voice that sounded like a poor imitation of a girl's voice.

"Messy, dirty, smelly," squeaked another wednesday in the same high voice.

"Mean, awful, immature," chanted three of the wednesdays together in a girlish singsong.

"Loathsome, nasty, vile," chirped Ninety-nine from his corner.

"Gooooood-byyyyee," they all sang in a chipper falsetto chorus. All of them, that is, except Two, whose face had turned crimson.

"Enough!" Two shrieked furiously. His eyes narrowed to slits as he glared at Max. *"Watch yourself,"* he hissed.

Max was baffled. It was just a silly question that had popped into his head at the last second. Of course, he *had* wondered why all of the wednesdays were boys, but that wasn't the most critical piece of information. He would have been better off asking where they went the rest of the week, or something about how the mind's mind worked.

"Goooooood-byyyyyeee," the other wednesdays sang again, softer this time. Even the older members of the

Tribunal joined in. Two lashed out, flinging several wednes-days violently to the floor.

An idea crept into Max's mind. Was it possible that the girl wednesdays had left because they were so disgusted with Two? It dawned on him that this could be important: he had stumbled onto a weakness in Two's authority. Max mentally filed away Two's reaction. It might just come in handy some-day. Two bared his teeth and roared to regain control over the group. This time, the other wednesdays obeyed him. They fell silent with their eyes once more averted.

"Ah, yes. The girls." Two brushed himself off prissily, act-ing as if nothing extraordinary had just happened. "Lovely creatures, all of them. Following a slight . . . misunderstand-ing, shall we say, about, ahem, management styles, the girls opted out of our happy little wednesday family here. We haven't seen them in over a hundred years. Tragic, really. I, for one, miss them terribly."

Max opened his mouth to ask another question, but Two interrupted him, rather rudely.

"Let's continue with the punishments, shall we?" Two snapped his fingers impatiently.

Three hesitated for a fraction of a second, but then shuf-fled over to the next wednesday sentenced by the Tribunal. He shoved Ninety-eight into the center of the room and then lurched back to his spot in the ring.

Two gestured at Max to begin the punishment. "Remember, Max, if you can't do it, then *I* will."

Ninety-eight looked pleadingly at Max, but this time Max knew better than to stare back or even to focus too intently on anything at all. He was ready to try out a new approach. He tried not to let any particular action or plan enter into his thoughts; in fact, he banished all thoughts of Ninety-eight from his mind altogether. Instead, Max simply stared straight at Two, narrowing his own eyes in response to Two's threatening glare. He didn't so much as blink, nor did he lower his eyes, even as Two bared his mossy teeth and ran his leathery tongue over one of his sharp fangs.

In his mind Max replayed what he was now sure was an imitation of the long-gone girl wednesdays: *silly, messy, dirty, smelly, mean, awful, immature, loathsome, nasty, vile*. It certainly sounded like an accurate description of Two.

Two started to fidget slightly under the strength of Max's stare. Just as Two looked to be ready to take a step back, a small voice that sounded very much like his own echoed in Max's head. "*Gotcha,*" whispered the voice in Max's mind, just as everything went crazy in the Council room.

CHAPTER 20

The hanging lightbulbs feebly illuminating the grimy room flickered and swayed, and objects began to fly around chaotically. A great bolt of electricity flared out from one of the dangling lights and connected briefly with Two, making him yelp in surprise. The room went pitch black, and Max heard the sound of heavy objects dropping all around him. Something papery fluttered by his ear, and something wet dripped on his cheek.

Finally, there was silence.

After what felt like an eternity, the lights flickered back on. The room was in utter shambles. The shelves had all collapsed, boxes were turned upside down, and paint in various shades of institutional beige was splattered everywhere.

Amidst the topsy-turvy mess, Two was cowering meekly in a corner. His hair was slightly singed, and his eyes were squeezed shut. He slowly opened first one eye, then the other, and then jumped to his feet as he realized that everyone was staring at him. "You'll pay for this," he growled at Max, but for once he didn't sound convincing at all. In fact, Max thought that he sounded almost . . . scared.

Wide-eyed, Max surveyed the damage to the room. *I did this?* He was starting to feel a bit proud of himself until he saw what had happened to Ninety-eight.

The poor wednesday was standing stiffly, as if afraid to move. His eyes brimmed with tears, and he was moaning quietly in pain. Max had to look closely to see what the mat-

ter was: an entire carton of pushpins had launched itself at Ninety-eight, literally turning him into a wednesday pincushion. Max rushed over and began pulling out the pushpins as Ninety-eight whimpered pitifully. One of them had narrowly missed his eye.

Max felt awful. He hadn't meant to actually *hurt* anyone.

That did it. He resolved to make his next question count, and this time he knew exactly what to ask. He pulled out a few more tacks and then turned toward the front of the room. "I'd like to ask my next question now."

Two, who had been huddled in deep conversation with several of the largest, ugliest Tribunal members, turned on him slowly. "Here's your answer, Max," he hissed. "But it's one you won't like. We wednesdays lie. We lie a lot. We quite *like* to lie."

"But I haven't even asked my question yet," Max protested. "You don't even know what I planned to ask."

"But I answered you already, and since an answer always follows a question, we're obviously done here." Two leered at him mockingly.

"That's absurd!" Max stomped his foot angrily. "It doesn't make a bit of sense, and besides—we had a deal."

Two raised one bristly, crusty eyebrow. "Well, then," he sniffed. "Since you clearly aren't satisfied with the terms of our arrangement, I will relieve you of your next sentencing duty." His eyes narrowed evilly as he pointed a crooked, clawed finger at Ninety-nine, who was desperately trying to hide behind one of the taller wednesdays. "Ninety-nine, for your crimes I hereby sentence you to two minutes of Tuesday." He gestured toward Max. "You have *him* to thank."

Ninety-nine cried out briefly, then collapsed to the floor in a faint. The other wednesdays looked stunned. Even Three seemed surprised. "*Two* minutes?" he asked the leader.

Two didn't answer. He turned abruptly on his heel and stalked out of the room in his strange, stumpy-legged way, leaving behind the distinct smell of burnt hair.

The rest of the wednesdays filed out of the room slowly; two of them had to half drag Ninety-nine, who was awake, but still shaky on his feet.

Only Ninety-eight and Max remained in the dusty storeroom. Max helped Ninety-eight pull the remaining pushpins out of his back, although, with his long wednesday arms, Ninety-eight didn't really need help reaching anything. The creature moaned woefully.

"I really am sorry, Ninety-eight," Max pleaded. "I truly didn't mean for you to get hurt."

"You do know that it was all a trick, don't you?" The wednesday was sulking now.

Max looked at him questioningly.

"Two tricked you, dummy," Ninety-eight said petulantly. "I tried to warn you. Every time you use your mind's mind, it gets stronger. The more you use it, the more wednesday you become. Eventually it just takes over, and you become like *them*—like us. It's been going on for weeks now, but you're just too dense to see what's been happening to you."

Max sank to the floor, stunned. If this was true, then he'd been played quite the fool. It had never even crossed his mind that Two had tricked him into using his new power.

"It's not a 'power,'" he corrected himself out loud. "It's a curse."

Max looked over his shoulder to make sure that they were still alone in the room, and then leaned over to whisper in Ninety-eight's ear. "Where do you go when it's not Wednesday?"

"There's Wednesday, and then there's not-Wednesday. On not-Wednesdays, there are not wednesdays," Ninety-eight answered cryptically, and Max could tell that the creature was still angry at him.

"But Ninety-nine was just sentenced to two minutes of Tuesday. Tuesday is obviously not Wednesday, so what does that mean?" Max was determined to get an answer. He suspected that finding out where they hid, or slept, or whatever it was they did six days a week, was the key to curing his case of the wednesdays.

"Oh, poor Ninety-nine," breathed Ninety-eight sadly. "Two minutes of Tuesday means that he has to be a wednesday on a not-Wednesday."

"I get that," Max said, frustrated, "but what does it *mean?*"

"It doesn't *mean* anything; it just *hurts.*" Ninety-eight shivered. "It's like having your skin ripped off and your eyeballs poked and your throat pulled out your nose and—"

"Okay, okay, I get it," Max interrupted him. "It hurts."

"Not-Wednesday is the very worst possible kind of punishment." The wednesday looked frightened just talking about it.

Max thought about this for a moment. "But," he began slowly, "Two said the girl wednesdays decided to leave the wednesday family. Wouldn't that mean they had chosen something else? Something not-Wednesday?"

"They didn't *choose* anything," Ninety-eight corrected him. "Two banished them. He closed the door."

Max wasn't getting anywhere at all. He desperately needed information, but every time he asked a question, he ended up even more confused by the answer.

"Sing him the song."

The quiet voice seemed to come from out of nowhere.

Ninety-eight acted as if he hadn't heard anything, but Max could see that he had.

"The song. Let's sing it for him." It was Ninety-nine. Max hadn't heard him enter the room, so he didn't know how much he had overheard.

Ninety-eight hesitated, still upset with Max, but he finally relented. Together, he and Ninety-nine sang a joyless tune:

A wednesday's job is never done
As long as Wednesdays are.
We heed the clock when it tolls twelve

And come from near and far.
We're never late—we cannot be—
For then we'd miss the door.
Neither do we dare to leave
Till Wednesday is no more.

Ninety-nine had crept out of his corner to sing the song, and he met Max's eyes boldly. Max was struck—not for the first time, either—with the strong feeling that there was still some small part of the creature that wasn't completely wednesday yet. And now, this not-wednesday part of Ninety-nine was trying to send him an important message. He paid careful attention to the song, searching for hidden meaning.

Just as they finished singing, Three poked his ugly, scarred face into the room and growled. The two smaller wednesdays scampered out past him, and singing time was over.

Max, who had had quite enough of the wednesdays that day, decided that it was a good time to head home. Three stood in his way menacingly, clearly trying to intimidate him. As Max pushed past, another bolt of electricity sparked briefly from the dangling lightbulb, zapping Three with a jolt that made the creature dance on his toes for a fraction of a second.

Max chuckled and kept walking. He hadn't *really* meant to do anything mean to Three, but neither did he feel sorry. Not one bit.

CHAPTER 21

Max glanced at his watch as he headed home. It was still several hours before midnight. He didn't know what to do until it was safe to go inside, and he was also feeling more than a little sorry for himself.

As he shuffled across the deserted town square he heard a voice calling in the distance. He froze in his tracks, not wanting to deal with yet another wednesday confrontation. Fortunately, it was only Mr. Grimsrud calling for his dog.

"Thursday! Thursday? It's time for supper, little fellow." Max heard Mr. Grimsrud before he spotted him.

The old man was limping about frantically, knocking on his head every second or third step. When he saw Max, he lurched over to him quickly. "I almost didn't recognize you without the blue skin," he said. "Have you seen my little dog?"

Max had not, but he promised to keep a lookout for him. "Mr. Grimsrud?" he asked hesitantly. "Why do *you* think the wednesdays leave you alone?"

The old man was distracted; his eyes continued to scan for his lost dog as he spoke to Max. "I don't know, lad. Like I told you, I've never even seen one."

"Because I was wondering if maybe it might have something to do with the metal plate in your head."

"Oh, it could be, but trust me, you don't want one of these in your noggin," Mr. Grimsrud told him, "no matter how pretty they sound when you knock on them. A boy your age wouldn't much like what you have to go through to get one. War's not much fun at any age, come to think of it." His expression turned melancholy.

Max sighed. He just wanted to find something— *anything*—that could help him to stop turning into a wednesday.

Mr. Grimsrud was about to walk away when he turned back to Max. "I do still have my old army helmet, though— it's made of steel. I don't know what good it'll do, but you're welcome to it."

Max nodded gratefully. He'd try anything.

Mr. Grimsrud instructed Max where to find the old helmet. "I'd accompany you, but I need to keep looking for Thursday. He's never run off for this long before. If I didn't know better, I'd say those wednesday critters were baiting him."

They parted ways and Max headed over to Mr. Grimsrud's cottage on the outskirts of town. Mr. Grimsrud had warned him that the helmet would be very dirty and probably rusty, too, since he had been using it as a flowerpot for years.

Max found the helmet near the ramshackle cottage's front stoop. It wasn't the only unusual item being used as a planter—the weedy yard also contained a chipped bathtub sprouting sunflowers, an ancient boot with mushrooms popping out between the laces, and a porcelain toilet containing a struggling tomato vine.

The shadows cast by the fading daylight against the sagging house gave Max the creeps, so he quickly replanted the cabbage flower that had been growing in the helmet. He shook the dirt and earthworms out of the helmet as well as he could before putting it on his head and then hurried away, eager to test out the effects of steel.

He made it all the way home without a single Wednesday mishap. He didn't trip over, step in, or get hit on the head by anything at all; his clothing remained intact; no birds or insects dive-bombed him; and as far as he could tell, nothing around him broke, went flat, or shattered. Was it a coincidence? His hopes rose slightly at the prospect of the helmet protecting him against the wednesdays.

Or, he realized grimly, it could just be that the wednesdays were too busy plotting against him at that moment.

Max hesitated when he reached his front door; he could hear baby Leland fussing inside as usual. It was dinnertime, and his parents were probably just sitting down at the table to eat. His mother had left a sandwich and a glass of milk out for him on the front step. Instead of eating outside, though, he took a deep breath, picked up the food, and entered the house.

"Oh, hello, dear," his mother said nervously, clutching at her napkin.

"Max!" his father called out, glancing at his watch in surprise.

Neither of his parents looked thrilled to see him. Baby Leland, on the other hand, stared at him adoringly. His howl quieted to a whimper, and then a hiccup.

"I know that it's not midnight yet, but I'd like to try something new," Max said hopefully. "I may have found something to help keep the wednesdays away." He explained Mr. Grimsrud's metal plate and pointed to the steel army helmet on his head. "I'll leave if anything bad starts to happen."

Max sat down at the dinner table and tried not to be offended as his parents inched away from him slightly.

They ate cautiously and silently, taking small bites and tiny sips. All of them jumped when the village clock tolled seven.

Nothing spilled. No one choked. The lights stayed on. Nothing caught on fire.

Bits of soil were still making Max's scalp itch miserably, but he didn't dare remove the helmet. Not when everything was going so well.

Max's father brought in bowls of ice cream for dessert; his hand trembled slightly as he poured tea for himself and Max's mother. Still, no one spoke.

Finally, Max's mother blotted her mouth and then laid her folded napkin down on the table. "Is it possible?" she asked in a whisper.

No one answered. It was as if they were all afraid to even hope that the helmet had cured Max.

They watched television together in silence, and when their program had ended, they said a hushed, wide-eyed good-night. On his way up the stairs, though, Max's father stumbled slightly. Max and his mother both cried out.

"No, no. It wasn't a Wednesday thing at all," his father quickly reassured them. He sheepishly held up a slipper that had been lying on one of the steps. "I forgot to put this away, and I tripped over it. Entirely my fault."

They all sighed with relief.

Max crept into bed, where he didn't sleep a wink—in fact, he barely breathed—until the clock said it was one minute past midnight. Then and only then did he fall into an exhausted slumber.

CHAPTER 22

After a blissfully uneventful breakfast, Max's parents decided that he should go back to school.

"But, Mom, the principal said I was a public health menace," Max protested, even though he really did want to go back. He hadn't been sorry to avoid math class for the last few days, but he wanted his normal life back, even if that meant geometry homework.

"Don't you worry about that, dear. I'll take care of him." His mother had a determined frown on her face.

"Here you go, good as new." His father handed him the now–sparkling clean army helmet, which he had cheerfully polished in his basement workshop. "The grime came right off with a good scrubbing."

Max groaned slightly at the sight of it. He knew *exactly* how the other kids at school were going to react to him showing up to class wearing the helmet, but he put it on anyway and steeled himself against the ridicule that it was sure to bring.

When they arrived at school, Max's mother instructed him to wait outside Mr. Alderwood's office. She squared her shoulders, arranged her face into a determined scowl, and then strode into the principal's office without even knocking.

Max could hear raised voices coming from behind the closed door, but he couldn't quite make out what was being said. His mother's voice was much louder than the principal's, though—that much was definitely clear.

Eventually, the door opened and his mother emerged, now bearing a victorious smile. Mr. Alderwood followed, his face beet red.

"Max, dear, the principal will personally escort you to class to be sure there are no more . . . *misunderstandings*." She shot a threatening look at Mr. Alderwood, kissed Max on the cheek, and then strode briskly out of the school.

Giving Max a wide berth, Mr. Alderwood marched him sternly down the hall toward homeroom.

"Phew. Your mother's a tough one, all right, isn't she?" Mr. Alderwood didn't seem to actually expect an answer, so Max just kept quiet.

The classroom immediately fell silent when Max

entered. The principal whispered something to Mrs. Trimersnide, who shook her head violently at whatever he was saying. They engaged in a hushed debate that ended only when the principal raised his hands in the air and said, "I don't like it any more than you do, Mary."

Looking distinctly relieved to be rid of his burden, Mr. Alderwood scampered out the door, leaving Max standing alone at the front of the silent classroom.

For several excruciating moments, the only sound in the room was the ticking of the clock. Several students cleared their throats nervously, and several more shifted awkwardly in their seats. No one met Max's eyes. No one spoke.

Finally, a lone voice from the back called out rudely, "Nice helmet!"

At last, the tension was broken. Max grinned gratefully at the culprit—Noah, of course. Hopefully this meant that his best friend wasn't angry at him for the radiator incident.

The room dissolved into twitters of nervous laughter, questions, and greetings.

With a sour look on her face, Mrs. Trimersnide shushed the room. "Calm down, everyone. Max, don't bother with your assigned seat. Today you sit in the back of the room. The *very* back. I'm warning you, though. Just *one* incident and I don't care what the principal says. . . ." The rest of her threat remained unspoken.

Max happily took the empty seat next to Noah, who leaned over and rapped twice on his helmet. It made a cheerful gonging sound. *Maybe Mr. Grimsrud was right*, Max thought. The sound *was* sort of soothing.

Mrs. Trimersnide reluctantly resumed her lesson, keeping one wary eye on Max at all times.

A folded-up note sailed through the air, landing at Max's feet. He looked up in surprise when he realized it had been sent by Gemma Swift. Max was trying to figure out how to retrieve the note without Mrs. Trimersnide noticing when he heard a loud creak, followed by a sharp splintering sound.

It sounded an awful lot like Wednesday.

• • •

Now, Mrs. Trimersnide was a large woman. She had the type of figure that Max's grandmother called "generous." Students called her "Mrs. Two-yards-wide" behind her back . . . and they weren't exaggerating by much.

As Max protested later, a woman Mrs. Trimersnide's size simply had no business sitting on the corner of school furniture built with smaller-statured users in mind. And yet, she had long been in the habit of perching her bulk precariously on the edge of the desk while she taught, ignoring the creaks and groans that sounded from the wood.

It was Max's misfortune that on this day, of all days, the heavily burdened desk finally gave out. One of the desk's spindly legs snapped, sending Mrs. Trimersnide and all of the desk's contents tumbling to the floor. Books, papers, an oversize stapler, a lone apple, and a glass paperweight slid to the ground; the paperweight shattered, and glass fragments flew everywhere.

Mrs. Trimersnide struggled to her feet, looking down in horror at a long run in her stockings. She turned her angry glare to the classroom, as if daring the students to laugh. No one dared.

Her mouth opened and closed several times, but no sound came out. Her face turned pink, then red, then purple, and her whole body seemed to puff up. She looked like a mighty volcano, ready to erupt.

And then she erupted. "You!" she thundered at Max. "You . . . wednesday! Get out! Get out of my classroom this instant!"

"But—but—" Max stammered, as surprised as she was by her fall. "But I didn't do it! It really wasn't me this time. It was because . . ." He stopped himself, realizing that he was in a no-win situation. As he stood up to leave, though, Noah leapt to his defense, finishing Max's sentence for him.

"It's because you're so *fat*!"

All around them, students' jaws dropped and eyes bulged in disbelief. Max couldn't believe his ears.

"Both of you. Principal's office. NOW!" Mrs. Trimersnide's voice rose to a shriek. "NOW!!"

Max and Noah took the hint. They grabbed their backpacks and fled for the hall; even as the door closed behind them, they heard the classroom erupt into a cacophony of shouts and laughter, followed by more shrieking from the enraged teacher.

They waited until they had made it around the corner before dissolving into hysterical laughter. "I can't believe you said that," Max exclaimed once he had caught his breath.

"That desk has been on the verge of collapse since my brother was in her class five years ago," Noah said. "It's not fair for you to take the blame." He paused for a moment. "You *didn't* do it, did you?"

Max reassured him that his helmet kept the wednesdays away. "No, it wasn't me, I swear it."

Noah looked relieved. "I believe you. But Mrs. Trimersnide sure won't." He snickered again.

The two boys made their way to Mr. Alderwood's office. The frazzled principal didn't look the least bit surprised to see them.

CHAPTER 23

"It's hard to explain." Max and Noah sat glumly on a curb in the village square, aimlessly tossing pebbles at an empty soda can several yards away. Max had done his best to describe his interactions with the wednesdays, as well as what had been happening to him, but Noah seemed skeptical.

Clink. "That's ten in a row for me," Noah said without enthusiasm as he hit his target. "You're zero for, like, a hundred, Max. It's no fun if you won't even try." He frowned. "I don't understand why you can't just hide from the wednesdays like the rest of us. Won't they leave you alone if you stay indoors for a few days?"

Max shrugged. His heart wasn't in the contest, and Noah's questions were making him feel worse than ever. "I guess it's too late for that. Trust me, I'd be willing to try anything to get rid of them, but nothing seems to be working." He tossed several more pebbles at the can, missing each time. "Sorry I got you suspended from school," he said finally. "On top of what happened to your house and all."

"Ah, it wasn't your fault," Noah replied generously. "Besides, it's like getting an extra-long weekend."

"Maybe for you. They aren't letting *me* back in on Monday." Max thought the principal was being terribly unfair.

"Tell you what. If you can manage to hit the can five times in a row, I'll play hooky on Monday and keep you company."

Max just shrugged again. He appreciated Noah's attempt to cheer him up, but it wasn't working. He had too much on his mind. Besides, he'd already gotten his friend in enough trouble.

The village clock tolled eleven, reminding Max that he had a doctor's appointment. The ringing of the tall clock, which had been built in the town's center over a hundred years earlier, also sparked another thought. "Noah, I have to go, but can you meet me here at the clock tomorrow? If you don't get into too much trouble with your parents, that is?"

Noah waved off his concern. "I'll be here. You're the most interesting thing that's happened in this village in . . . well, in forever. But you better tell me *everything* next time I see you. Or else . . ." He waggled his fist even as he grinned at Max.

Max promised and then raced off toward the doctor's office as fast as his legs could carry him. He walked in just in time to hear the tail end of his mother's lecture to Dr. Tetley. ". . . I should report you for invasion of privacy! Isn't my son entitled to patient confidentiality just like everyone else?" Dr. Tetley, who seemed to have shrunk under the weight of the tirade, mumbled something inaudible and then slunk out of his own office, leaving Max and his mother with Dr. Conkle-Smoak.

Max's mother noticed the parapsychologist for the first time. "Oh, for goodness' sake," she muttered, shaking her head in disbelief as she saw what he was wearing. "Is that getup really necessary?"

Dr. Conkle-Smoak seemed genuinely surprised that she would disapprove of his frayed velvet robe. "Madam, I re-quire a garment upon which I can display my honorary re-galia."

To Max's eyes, the robe looked suspiciously like a bath-robe, and the doctor's "honorary regalia" looked a lot like Boy Scout badges. Instead of Boy Scout symbols, though, Dr. Conkle-Smoak's pins and patches had pictures of vari-ous astral signs and crystal formations.

"Let's just get on with this." Max's mother wore the same

expression she usually had when she was suffering from a migraine.

Dr. Conkle-Smoak asked Max a series of questions that ranged from bizarre to outrageous; he took notes with a feather-tipped pen.

"Which eye do you open first when you wake—the left or the right?"

He insisted that Max's answer of "both of them together" couldn't possibly be correct.

"Can you feel your hair growing now?"

Max had to think about that for a moment before he responded.

"Have you recently had any dreams involving a jack-o'-lantern, a steamship, or a miniature orangutan?"

He seemed puzzled to hear that Max had not.

Dr. Conkle-Smoak then examined Max's tongue very carefully—even drawing a detailed diagram of it in his notes—before asking anything specific about the wednesdays. His eyes widened when Max described the mood ring color changes, and he enthusiastically scribbled pages of notes. "I'm going to have to consult my manuals for that," he murmured.

Max's mother snorted, but didn't otherwise comment.

The doctor grew even more interested when Max told him about the metal plate in Mr. Grimsrud's head and his theory that the steel army helmet seemed to be reducing his wednesday symptoms. "*Fascinating*. And I thought your helmet was just a flash of sartorial genius. It made me fancy a visit to the haberdasher."

Max had no idea what Dr. Conkle-Smoak was talking about.

The doctor continued excitedly. "But, really, it makes perfect sense when you think about it."

It does? Max was having trouble following the strange man's ramblings.

"Of course it does. It all comes down to magnets. I should have thought to measure your magnetic meridian, but it just seemed too obvious, too basic. But you see, by wearing the steel helmet, you are effectively blocking transcranial radiance. You've clearly altered your bioelectromagnetic field sufficiently to prevent these . . . wednesdays, as you call them, from influencing your psycho-vibrational perimeter."

"So, this all makes sense to you?" Max was skeptical.

"Oh, yes—it's all quite elementary. These are the same simple principles used in basic time travel science." Dr. Conkle-Smoak was so busy scribbling notes that he didn't notice Max's mother cradling her head in her hands and slumping dejectedly in her chair.

"So, does that mean there's a cure?" Max asked hopefully.

"Well, I must confess that it has been quite some time

since I finished my correspondence course in radiesthesia, but with intensive polarity therapy, I think we might eventually be able to restore you to normal psychic radiation levels."

Max's mother jumped to her feet when she heard this. "*Radiation levels?* Don't you dare go anywhere near my son with anything radioactive! I won't allow it."

The doctor politely gestured for her to sit back down. "Well, that *would* be the most direct course of treatment, madam, but if you are not inclined to give your consent, then I believe that we can still be effective even if we limit ourselves to therapeutic magnetism."

She sat back down, muttering under her breath. Max heard the words *lunatic* and *deranged*, but she didn't interrupt again.

"Fortunately for you, I brought my field equipment along." Dr. Conkle-Smoak hoisted a large canvas pack onto his back. "Shall we?" he asked, gesturing to the door with a dramatic flourish of his floor-length robe.

CHAPTER 24

The robe-clad parapsychologist fiddled with a small box that looked suspiciously like an old-fashioned television remote control with a long antenna glued onto it. Dr. Conkle-Smoak was standing in the gazebo in the center of the village, waving the device in front of him like a metal detector.

"All readings are neutral here. Are you absolutely certain this is the first place you encountered a wednesday?" The doctor shook the device roughly, but it remained silent.

Max nodded. They had wanted to go take measurements from the storage room underneath the bleachers in the school gymnasium, but since Max had been officially banned from the school grounds, they had to start somewhere else.

"Wait just a minute." The doctor froze, and then sniffed deeply. "I think I smell their urine. If I can collect a sample, I could run tests on it."

"Oh, no—that's probably just from Thursday. He likes to . . . go here." Max remembered that Mr. Grimsrud's ugly dog had marked his spot on the gazebo steps the last time he was there.

"I thought you said they were called wednesdays?" Dr. Conkle-Smoak looked confused.

"They are," Max answered impatiently. "Thursday isn't a wednesday; he's a dog."

The doctor continued to look confused.

"There *is* another place we could try," Max said slowly.

He led the way to the clock tower in the center of the town square. He was positive that Ninety-nine had been trying to tell him something important when he sang the wednesday song, and one of the song's lines included a reference to a clock. The tower was the tallest building in the village by a considerable margin, and Max stood at the base, looking up as he recited the lyrics to the doctor:

A wednesday's job is never done
As long as Wednesdays are.
We heed the clock when it tolls twelve
And come from near and far.
We're never late—we cannot be—
For then we'd miss the door.
Neither do we dare to leave
Till Wednesday is no more.

"I was planning to come back later to look for some sort of a door on the clock," Max explained.

"Dear boy, if there's one thing that I've learned from my study of parapsychology, it's that you should never take things too literally—wait a minute. I'm getting a reading! I'm getting an enormous reading here! The level of cosmo-telluric energy here is positively ethereal!" Dr. Conkle-Smoak was so excited that he sprayed spittle as he spoke.

Max's mother, who had not said a single word since they left the office, sighed mournfully and pulled a handkerchief from her purse to wipe the spittle off her cheek. "And this means *what*, exactly?" She sounded utterly unmoved by the discovery.

"Mom, this is important," Max urged. "One of the wednesdays—one of the nicer ones, that is—was trying to tell me something important about this clock. We need to get inside this tower."

Unfortunately, they could not enter the building. Max

did find a small metal door, painted a scabby shade of mauve, on the side of the tower, but it was locked. He tried removing his helmet and using his wednesday powers to break down the door, but the only thing that happened was that a bluebird flew directly into the wall of the clock tower.

"Sorry," Max whispered to the dazed bird lying on the ground. He quickly put his helmet back on his head.

"I'm going to march over to city hall this minute to find someone to let us in," Max's mother declared.

As she left, Dr. Conkle-Smoak removed a small vial from his pocket and knelt down to fill it with a sample of the soil at the base of the clock tower. "Extraordinary," he muttered to himself.

"Did you find something?" Max asked excitedly.

"What? Oh, no, nothing like that. I was just thinking about how extraordinarily delicious my breakfast pastry was this morning. Oh, wait—what's this?" The doctor bent stiffly to examine something low to the ground, his knees popping loudly in protest. He pulled out a sheet of paper and a pencil, and then proceeded to rub the pencil over the paper as he held it against one of the building's bricks. "There's a faint engraving here. Let's see what it says."

Max peered at the image the pencil rubbing revealed on the paper. Several words appeared in an antiquated script:

Psyche Pannuchizein Exodo

"What does it mean?"

"I'm afraid that I flunked the ancient languages semester of my schooling. I'll have to look it up later." Looking slightly embarrassed, the doctor stuffed the pencil rubbing into his pocket. Next, he filled three more vials with soil, and then stuck his tongue out and proceeded to thoughtfully lick the wall.

Max watched, baffled, as he tasted each wall of the tower.

"There's a saying that we parapsychologists have," he explained. "North, south, east, west, the spirit world tastes the best."

"So you can tell where they come in and out of the clock?" Max was starting to think the strange doctor might actually be on to something.

"They use the door, it seems." Dr. Conkle-Smoak did not sound certain. "At least, the door tastes considerably better than the walls. Give it a try."

• • •

Max's mother returned to find Max licking the bricks on the clock tower's east side. "Maxwell Valentino Bernard! What on earth are you doing?"

"Nothing," Max said sheepishly, not wanting to explain. All of the walls, and the door as well, tasted more or less the same, as far as he could tell. If anything, the door just tasted slightly rustier than the walls.

"Blasted bureaucracy!" His mother was livid. "The ninny working at city hall told me that I had to file a formal request for permission to enter the clock tower, and that it would have to be approved at the next city council meeting at the end of the month."

That's too late, Max thought. He hadn't told anyone about the week of Wednesdays yet. Everyone was treating him so differently already; if they knew he was only a short time away from becoming a wednesday forever, they'd be even more afraid to be around him. He'd have to find some other way into the clock tower on his own.

"Come along, then, Max, if we're done here," his mother said, checking her watch. "I need to get home to feed baby Leland."

Dr. Conkle-Smoak promised to get back to them as soon as possible once he had completed his analysis of the samples and the field readings. Max could only hope that the doctor actually knew what he was doing, since no one else seemed to understand what was happening to him.

CHAPTER 25

Noah was already waiting at the base of the clock tower when Max arrived the next morning.

"How'd you manage to get out? I thought your parents would chain you up in your basement once they heard that you were suspended from school." Max sat down with his friend on the curb, relieved to have someone to share the day with.

"Nah," Noah said easily. "For starters, the basement is still off-limits till they fix the boiler, no thanks to you. My folks are so busy with the repairs they'll never even notice I'm gone."

Max ducked his head sheepishly, more grateful than ever that Noah wasn't one to hold a grudge.

"But if I'm going to spend the rest of the month doing all my sisters' chores in addition to my own for that little stunt you pulled at my house on Wednesday, then you'd better start talking. I want to hear *everything*." Noah waved his finger in Max's face jokingly. "*And* you're buying ice cream for me every afternoon this week to make up for me losing TV privileges thanks to the suspension."

"Deal." Max wasn't about to protest Noah's demands. He'd have agreed to almost anything just to have someone to talk to about the last week's events. He had just started to fill Noah in on the details of his run-ins with the wednesdays when they heard a loud throat-clearing noise behind them.

Max jumped; his first reaction was to panic—to worry that the wednesdays had somehow found him, even though it was a Friday. His panic actually increased when he saw that it was Gemma Swift standing behind them. "G-G-Gemma. Why aren't you in school?" He hated himself for stammering, but something about her always made him feel nervous and clumsy. She was just so . . . intense.

She rolled her eyes. "School's for amateurs. I'm taking a sick day. As in, I'm sick of school. Besides, I'm writing a story for the school newspaper about this wednesday business, and I need a quote from you."

Max started to object—the last thing on earth he needed was the kind of attention a newspaper article was sure to bring—but Gemma cut him off. "I had a feeling that you might not want to talk to a reporter, so I brought something

along to change your mind. I heard you might need this."
She was twirling a single key on a long chain.

Max and Noah just looked at her blankly. "What is it?"
Noah asked finally.

Gemma gave an exasperated sigh. "Duh. It's the master key to all of the village municipal buildings." When the boys still looked confused, she sighed again. "It will open the clock tower. My dad told me that you had applied for access. The city council will take forever, so I just . . . borrowed this key from my dad's desk drawer. He'll never notice."

It suddenly became clear to Max. Gemma's father was the village mayor. He ran everything and knew everyone; of course he would have the keys to the clock. Max felt himself blushing slightly, though. First, Peter's dad had spilled the beans about his case of the wednesdays, and now Gemma's dad had told her all about the clock. "Is it completely *impossible* to keep anything secret in this village?" he asked irritably.

Fortunately, Noah was there to remind him of his manners via a sharp elbow in the ribs. "Aren't you going to say thank you?" he prompted Max.

He was right. Max quickly wiped the scowl off his face and thanked Gemma. She smiled back confidently and joined the boys on the curb. "Okay, Max. Start from the beginning," she commanded. "Tell us what happened."

● ● ●

Neither of Max's new partners in crime said a word until he finished talking. But once he was done, they peppered him with questions.

"So, why haven't you met One yet?" Gemma looked skeptical. "And are there actually any girl wednesdays? Where are they?"

"Who cares?" Noah interrupted. "All we need to know is how to get rid of them."

Max stopped them both. "There's a lot I don't understand. They're terribly confusing, if you haven't already guessed. And these last few weeks have been really, truly awful." It occurred to him that what he needed most from his friends at that moment was a bit of sympathy—an arm around the shoulders, perhaps, or even a proper hug, though he would most certainly never admit *that* out loud, especially around Noah.

It was a silly thought.

Gemma was too busy scribbling notes in a spiral notebook that she had pulled out of her purse.

Noah, on the other hand, had jumped up and started to pace. "Why don't we just get—I don't know, the police or the military, or the dogcatcher, or *someone*—to exterminate the nasty things? The whole village hates the wednesdays—

160

everyone would be glad to see them gone." His eyes sparkled as he began to plot the destruction of the creatures.

"It's more complicated than that," Max explained nervously. He hadn't let on yet that *he* was halfway to being a wednesday himself. "They're not all mean—just the older ones. And it's not like they chose to become wednesdays. I mean, I think they were normal kids who just happened to be chosen by Two. Or One. Or someone . . . I don't know. It's not their fault, really."

Noah wasn't convinced. "Ah, would you quit defending them, Max? They must have zapped your brain or something. Come on—don't go soft on us now!" He clapped Max on the back hard enough to make him sputter.

Gemma's eyes narrowed in suspicion. "You *do* sound as if you're defending them. You're obviously not telling us something. Fess up, Maxwell."

Max looked pleadingly at Noah for help, but Noah wasn't the least bit inclined to jump to his rescue on this point, at least. He crossed his arms over his chest, waiting to hear what Max had to say. "Go on—answer her. I'm curious, too. I want to know why my best friend is suddenly making excuses for the same little pests who replaced the ball bearings in my skateboard wheels with pebbles just last month. Do you have any idea how much that cost to fix?"

The thought of telling them—telling them *everything*—

filled Max with a combination of dread and relief. But he couldn't hold it in any longer. He just couldn't. He drew a long breath, and then told them his shameful secret.

"I'm . . . Next."

He tried to act as if it wasn't any sort of a big deal, but when he heard Gemma gasp and saw the look of deep concern on Noah's face, he felt tears prickling his eyes. Something about saying it out loud made it seem truly and terribly *real* for the first time.

"So, how much longer do you have?" Gemma whispered.

"As far as I can tell, a week of Wednesdays means seven Wednesdays. It's been three." Revealing the secret he had been carrying around wasn't easy for Max, but now that he was finally talking about it—*dealing* with it—he felt a weight lifting from his chest.

"Plenty of time," Noah said boldly. "But I still don't understand why we can't just wipe them out."

"Oh, that's kind of you, Noah." Gemma stood up for Max. "Really sensitive, considering your best friend is basically one of them."

Max started to protest, but he knew she was right. He slumped against the curb miserably.

"Sorry, Max," Noah mumbled. "I didn't mean *you.*"

"Well, let's get on with it, then," Gemma announced. She stood up and dusted herself off, then headed for the door on the rear wall of the clock tower.

Max and Noah exchanged shrugs, then followed. Gemma had a way of making people follow her.

"You two stay out here and keep watch. I'm not supposed to have the key, and I don't want to get in trouble for skipping school, either." Gemma turned the key in the lock.

"Maybe you shouldn't go alone," Max warned her. "Dr. Conkle-Smoak said the wednesday readings were"—he struggled to remember the correct term—"really high," he finished lamely. "They might be sleeping in there, for all we know."

Gemma rolled her eyes at him and then slipped through the door, leaving it open just a crack.

"What a woman," Noah whispered appreciatively as she disappeared.

Max paced back and forth, his eyes darting from the door to the deserted village square. He realized after a few moments that he had been holding his breath. Just as he exhaled, an ear-piercing scream sounded from inside the clock.

CHAPTER 26

Max V. Bernard might have had his faults—he tended to be untidy, and he was easily distracted, for starters. But it must be said that when he heard Gemma scream, Max reacted as quickly as anyone wearing a heavy steel helmet and increasingly ill-fitting clothing possibly could. Fortunately, or unfortunately, depending on your point of view, Noah reacted just as quickly.

"Gemma!" Max and Noah both leapt for the door at the exact same time, colliding roughly. Max's helmet fell off and rolled away; Noah then tripped over the helmet, hitting his head on the edge of the sidewalk with a frightful thud.

"My nose!" Noah's nose was gushing a tremendous flow of blood. Max hurriedly removed his sweatshirt so Noah could use it to stop the bleeding. No sooner had he thrust the garment against his friend's injured face than the door was violently flung open.

"Aaaarrgh! Ouch-ouch-ouch-ouch!" Gemma screamed again as she flew out the door, waving frantically at her hair. She slammed the door behind her, but it bounced back open, sending her tumbling to the ground.

Noah was shouting something, but his voice was muffled by the sweatshirt pressed against his nose, so Max couldn't understand a word. Noah removed the makeshift bandage just long enough to yell: "Put your helmet back on!"

Gemma shrieked yet again, this time at the sight of the rather impressive quantity of blood flowing from Noah's nose. Her own face was swelling rapidly on one side.

Horrified by what was happening all around him, Max rushed to retrieve his helmet. "What happened to your face?" he asked.

"Wasp sting," Gemma explained miserably.

"That's why you screamed?" Max asked.

"Well, the second time, yes. The first time I did it just as a joke, to scare you. There's nothing but clock parts inside," she admitted sheepishly. "And apparently also a wasps' nest."

Max insisted on seeing for himself. Watching out carefully for stray wasps, he crept inside. It was a tall, narrow building with a winding staircase climbing steeply to the clock at the top. Sunlight streamed in through decorative openings in the bricks, casting eerie shadows against the inner walls.

There weren't many hiding places. Wherever the wednesdays lived the other six days of the week, it certainly wasn't here. Just to be sure, he crept to the top of the staircase and studied the clock's gears and levers briefly. Under any other circumstances he would have spent more time looking at the complicated device, and maybe even tinkered with the chimes for fun. Today, though, he had no time for fun. If anything, the clock served as a great big reminder of just how little time he had before he turned into a wednesday forever.

A wasp buzzed by, looking for somewhere to land, or perhaps someone to sting. Max waved it off and then ran down the stairs. He might not have found any evidence, but he could *feel* the presence of the wednesdays here. His skin prickled and tingled, and his nose wrinkled at their noxious scent. He burst out the door, closing it behind him with a slam.

"What now?" Noah looked at him expectantly. But because he still had the sweatshirt pressed to his face, it sounded more like, "Wud no?"

"I wish I knew," Max wailed as he took in the sight of his bloodied, battered friends. For the first time since he encountered the wednesdays, he began to feel deeply despondent.

Fortunately, Gemma wasn't one to despair. "Snap out of it," she barked. "It's time for a plan. Let's list what we know for sure." She began to tick off items on her fingers, consulting her notepad for reference as she spoke. "First, their song talks about a clock and a door. Second, your psychic told you that he picked up definite readings here, right?"

"Parapsychologist," Max corrected her weakly, nodding.

"Whatever. Third, you look like you've seen a ghost, and you're practically hyperventilating, so this place is obviously affecting you. Well, either that or you're just a big coward, but I don't think that's the case. Finally—and don't take this the wrong way—your eyes are starting to look *really* bizarre."

Noah peered over the bloodstained sweatshirt to examine Max's eyes for himself. "Oh, she's right. They're . . . bigger and shinier or something. They *do* look weird." He scooted away from Max. "Creepy."

Max rubbed his eyes self-consciously. If they were already turning noticeably silver, then perhaps he was even further along in his transformation than he realized.

That very thought occurred to Gemma at the same instant. "Max," she asked in a gravely serious voice, "are you *absolutely certain* that you have four more Wednesdays left?"

But Max wasn't sure—he wasn't sure of anything at all. He had assumed that the week of Wednesdays started on the day that he first met the wednesdays. But what if it had started earlier? What if they had *targeted* him without his ever realizing it?

He blinked back tears and tried to swallow past the lump in his throat.

Once again, Gemma took charge of the situation. She really was unlike anyone else his age Max had ever met, and for the moment, he was grateful. "Well, you're here, and it's not Wednesday, so that must mean you're still *you* for now, at least. But we shouldn't take any chances. We need to be right here, at the clock, precisely at midnight on Wednesday to see if they appear."

This plan perked Noah up, and he nodded in agreement. "Yeah. We can be, like, your bodyguards or something, Max!" He crouched down and made karate-chopping motions in the air, which unfortunately made his nose begin to bleed even more.

"I can't let you do that," Max said reluctantly. "It's too risky. Besides, you've already done enough, Gemma. I'll give you a quote for your article and then you can go back to avoiding me like everyone else."

But instead of looking relieved, Gemma looked annoyed. "You can't get rid of me that easily, Max Bernard."

Max was confused. He'd thought that she'd be happy to get her quote and then be on her way. "Um, not to sound ungrateful, Gemma, but why do you even want to be involved anyway? You barely know me."

Gemma blushed slightly. "Is it so impossible to think that perhaps I'm just being nice?"

Max and Noah stared her down until she finally answered.

"Fine. If you insist, then I'll tell you. The thing is, this is all going to make the most absolutely incredible story. Forget the silly old school newspaper—this is *so* much bigger.

The local TV station will *definitely* want to interview me—I mean, us—and I need airtime for my portfolio. We might even get national coverage!"

"Portfolio?" Max still didn't understand.

"Don't be slow, Max. I'm going to be a television news reporter someday, and the more airtime I get now, the better my job prospects will be when I finish school." Gemma at least had the courtesy to look slightly embarrassed by her confession. "Please, Max, let me help? I really want this scoop! It truly is the most *amazing* story."

"Okay, fine." Max relented. "But I hope you both know what you're getting into." He couldn't help but feel slightly offended by Gemma's motives, but he also knew that he needed her help. In fact, he had a terrible feeling that he was going to need all the help he could get.

CHAPTER 27

"I'm afraid I bear unwelcome news." Dr. Conkle-Smoak greeted Max with a solemn expression on his face.

"What, you've misplaced your magic wand?" Max's mother's voice dripped with sarcasm.

The doctor frowned. "Madam, this is grave business indeed, and I encourage you to take your son's well-being more seriously."

Max watched as his mother's face flushed and she ducked her head in embarrassment. "I'm sorry. You're right," she said quietly.

"Make all the jokes at my expense that you want—I'm accustomed to it. But you need to be aware that the test results indicate that these wednesdays are thoroughly malevolent creatures. Their condition"—the doctor cleared his throat, and then looked directly into Max's eyes—"*your* condition . . . is progressive and irreversible."

"Irreversible?" Max cried out. "But that must be wrong. The helmet works—nothing bad happens when I wear the metal helmet."

Dr. Conkle-Smoak shook his head sadly. "An imperfect solution at best—a bit like wearing a raincoat in a flood. It's more likely that the only thing the helmet was doing was protecting your skull from the various projectiles those lousy little gremlins like to toss your way."

"But what about Mr. Grimsrud?" Max argued. "He has a metal plate in his head, and the wednesdays don't bother *him*."

"Ah, yes, Mortimer Grimsrud. He was a few grades ahead of me in school way back when; I know him well." Dr. Conkle-Smoak hesitated for a moment, as if unsure how much he wanted to share. "Unfortunately for you, my dear boy, Mr. Grimsrud has an advantage that you do not. You see, he is quite mentally unbalanced—has been since the war. Perhaps it's the combination of madness and metal that protects him, like some sort of special, metallurgical cocktail, but I'm only speculating here. The only thing that's clear is that you are getting worse every day."

Max wanted to protest further, but he knew the doctor was right. Small things had started to go wrong around him, almost as if he was leaking wednesday symptoms in spite of his helmet and in spite of his best efforts to keep his thoughts under control. He had resorted to singing a constant refrain of silly Christmas songs in his head to prevent himself from thinking any unkind thoughts that might end up hurting someone.

His mother began to cry softly. Max wanted to put his arms around her to comfort her, but he couldn't risk it. Earlier that morning she had burned her hand on a stove that she swore had been cool just a moment before. It had happened as soon as Max walked into the kitchen. At the time, he had hoped it was an unfortunate coincidence, but now he had to admit that it was probably something more sinister.

Dr. Conkle-Smoak pulled out a measuring tape and wrapped it around Max's head. He muttered under his breath as he took several more measurements of Max's limbs and then checked the figures against his notes from the previous week.

"It's different from last time, isn't it? I'm different." Max didn't even wait for the doctor to answer. He already knew. None of the clothes in his closet fit him properly anymore, and just that morning he had seen in the mirror that his head was

starting to look bigger and more squarish than normal. His reflection had made him think of Two's evil, mossy grin, and he had brushed his teeth more forcefully than necessary for several long minutes.

"I'm almost a wednesday," he whispered to himself.

"How much longer does he have, Doctor?" His mother was sobbing by now.

"It's hard to say, madam." Even the doctor had tears in his eyes. "A few weeks, give or take. But I can't be certain. This is all theoretical. I have scoured every book, contacted every colleague who could possibly know more than I do about this subject, and I've even consulted some of the . . . darker sources of knowledge. Unfortunately, no one seems to know anything at all about these wednesdays of yours."

A thought occurred to Max. "Dr. Conkle-Smoak," he began, "would it help if you could see the wednesdays for yourself? What I mean to ask is, would that possibly help you find a cure?"

The parapsychologist paled. "Oh, dear boy. I am a scientist, not a . . . soldier." He pulled at his ear nervously.

"Although . . ." He stopped to think. He pressed his index fingers to his temples violently, hunched his shoulders, and turned his back to Max and began to mutter.

He was talking to himself. Max exchanged a worried look with his mother, and then leaned forward so that he could make out what seemed to be a heated discussion between Dr. Conkle-Smoak and . . . himself.

"For alchemy's sake, good man. . . . This is your chance—think of the treatise you could write. You'd be the talk of the Esoteric Cosmology Convention this year. . . . Maybe even the keynote speaker!" The robed man shook one finger at himself and then the other.

For several minutes the doctor vigorously argued both sides, alternating between sudden loud exclamations such as "It's too risky, you fool!" and "Knowledge must prevail!"

Dr. Conkle-Smoak finally sighed deeply, then turned back to face Max. He mopped his brow, straightened his robe, and nodded gravely. "I have reached a decision. At great personal peril, I shall accompany you to make the acquaintance of these *wednesdays*." His voice cracked. "I am a scientist of the psyche, and I must treat the unknown as my laboratory. I cannot falter in my pursuit of the truth."

Max was surprised at the amount of relief he felt, even if his new ally did tend to be melodramatic and quite possibly slightly insane. "Thank you, Doctor," he said gratefully. "I'll do whatever I can to protect you from them."

As his mother cried in the corner as if her heart would break, Max instructed the doctor when and where to meet.

CHAPTER 28

The observers arrived at the clock tower within minutes of one another. As they crept from the shadows and gathered in the square, each of them glanced up fearfully at the silent clock, wondering if the lofty tower might really be just minutes away from belching up a group of monstrous creatures. Eyeing the time nervously, Gemma and Noah breathlessly compared stories about how they had managed to sneak out of their houses undetected. "I've never been out of the house on a Wednesday before," Noah said. He jumped slightly as the minute hand ticked forward a notch. "It already feels like an adventure, doesn't it?" He crouched down into his favorite karate stance and then shouted out at the top of his lungs: "Stay back, you lousy wednesdays, or I'll give you a taste of my kung fu!"

"It's not Wednesday yet," Dr. Conkle-Smoak chastised

him. The doctor was wearing a faded gray sweat suit under his velvet robe. He had dark circles under his eyes and looked as if he would much rather be at home in bed.

Max was already waiting for them when they arrived. He'd told everyone to be at the clock at ten minutes till midnight, but he arrived much earlier. He had needed the time to think. "Don't get too close to me," he cautioned the new arrivals. "I don't want anything bad to happen to you on account of my . . . wednesday-ness." He tossed a large duffel bag toward the others.

Noah looked confused as he pulled three metal mixing bowls out of the bag. "What, we're baking cookies for them now?"

"Sorry about that; I had to improvise a bit. I couldn't find any more helmets, so I brought those bowls and some duct tape. Use the tape to make a chin strap so you can wear the bowls on your head. It might look a bit silly, but it will hopefully give you at least some protection. Metal may not stop the wednesdays, but it at least shields your head from whatever they toss our way."

Max had spent the last few days making himself scarce. It was simply too stressful to watch terrible things happen to everyone around him, knowing it was all his fault. Hiding away might have made things easier, but in his self-imposed solitude he had found himself plagued by a constant stream of melancholy thoughts. *What if this is the last time I get to eat my mom's lasagna? What do wednesdays eat? What if I can't even remember anything from my normal life once I become a wednesday?*

His only comfort had come from planning and plotting.

"Listen carefully," he addressed the small group. "We only have a few minutes until midnight. Be sure your bowl helmets are taped on tight, don't touch any of the wednesdays, and try not to look them directly in the eye. Some of them are harmless enough, but the bigger and the uglier they look, the more dangerous they are. Watch out for the biggest one—the one with a giant scar across his face—that's Three, and he's incredibly strong. And no matter what you do, watch out for Two. He's meaner and more dangerous than the rest of them combined."

"How will we know which one is Two . . . ?" Noah trailed off as the clock tower started to glow with an eerie green light. A soft, humming noise seemed to be coming from the bricks themselves, and several bats flew out of the openings in the tower. Suddenly, the door burst open with a crash.

But it's not time yet! Max was startled to see a wednesday come hurtling out of the door as if the building was on fire. In fact, the creature was acting as if *he* was on fire, even though there were no visible flames. The wednesday was screaming and howling in terrible agony, clawing at his own face and skin. The dreadful noise was nearly unbearable to witness as the creature writhed and kicked on the ground. It didn't seem possible, but the screams continued to grow louder and louder.

Ninety-nine! Suddenly, it made sense to Max. Ninety-nine had been sentenced to two minutes of Tuesday. Max's eyes flew to the clock: it was 11:58.

"Oh, this is just horrible! Can't you make it stop?" Gemma cried out to no one in particular, her eyes filling with tears as she watched the creature's suffering.

"You're a doctor—do something!" Max shoved Dr. Conkle-Smoak toward the flailing, shrieking wednesday.

The doctor looked terrified as he approached Ninety-nine. He glanced over his shoulder, clearly hoping someone else would volunteer for the dangerous task.

"Help him," Gemma screamed, covering her face with her hands.

But just as Dr. Conkle-Smoak nervously reached out to the wednesday, he was thrown back with a powerful force. He landed on the ground several feet away and winced in pain as he examined his hand, which was quickly turning an angry shade of red.

Max saw what had happened, but as Ninety-nine continued to wail in agony, he couldn't just stand by and watch. He ran toward the small wednesday, but just as the parapsychologist had been thrown back, so was Max. He landed roughly on the sidewalk, his skin tingling painfully as if he had been burned. Noah wordlessly helped him to his feet.

For two long, terrible minutes, the group watched helplessly as Ninety-nine suffered. Gemma sobbed softly and turned away. Noah seemed frozen in place. Dr. Conkle-Smoak took out a pad of paper and sketched furiously, wincing from the pain in his hand. Max stared at the clock, silently pleading for the hands to move faster to put an end to Ninety-nine's torture.

It seemed to take an eternity, but the clock finally reached midnight, and the screaming ended as the bells began to toll. Max raced toward Ninety-nine at the first of the twelve strikes of the clock. This time he was able to approach without being burned or flung back.

Max was doing his best to comfort the traumatized wednesday, who lay moaning and shaking on the ground, when the glow from the clock tower grew brighter and the door creaked ever so slowly open. A single-file line of wednesdays, led by Two, began staggering out in numerical order. They were softly chanting the wednesday song, but their voices sounded listless and hoarse.

Two spotted Max and headed for him, but he was moving stiffly and slowly, as if just emerging from a long slumber.

"Quick, they're coming," Max whispered to Ninety-nine. "I need to know—how much longer do I have?"

The wednesday did not yet seem capable of speaking; he moaned unintelligibly.

"Please! Tell me before they get here!" Max crouched warily, prepared to run.

Ninety-nine looked fearfully at the slowly advancing wednesdays. Two drew a finger menacingly across his throat as a clear signal for the younger creature to remain silent. Max started to stand, figuring he'd never get his answer with Two so close, but Ninety-nine pulled him back down with surprising strength.

"The ceremony is next week. The Tribunal chose you six Wednesdays ago. Do whatever it takes. Don't let them get you. *Whatever it takes*," Ninety-nine whispered forcefully into Max's ear before slumping to the ground in an exhausted faint.

Max had what he needed. Two was still several feet away, but he was grinning evilly. "Hello, Next. You brought friends. How very thoughtful of you." His snake's hiss of a voice had a threatening tone that spurred Max into action. He had to protect his friends.

"Everybody, run!" Max yelled.

But Noah, loyal friend that he was, held his ground. "Give him back to us!" he shouted at the advancing creatures. "We won't let you take Max!"

Max grabbed his friend roughly by the shirt, spinning him around. "Not now, Noah! Run!"

As Max, Noah, and Gemma ran, a power line came crashing down in front of them, blocking their path. The live wire sparked and twisted dangerously, and Noah leapt out of the way just in time to avoid being electrocuted.

"Keep going, I'll meet you there!" Max had already instructed everyone to meet in his backyard if they became separated. This time they didn't argue—just nodded and ran on.

He looked back. Dr. Conkle-Smoak was slowly backing away from the wednesdays, but his attention was focused on the measurement tool that he was pointing at the creatures. The device was beeping wildly and shaking so violently that the doctor could barely hold on to it.

"Watch out!" Max saw that Three had separated from Two and was sneaking around behind Dr. Conkle-Smoak.

The doctor looked up and saw the trap. Instead of running, though, he began to rummage frantically through the pockets of his robe.

Max watched in horror as Two narrowed his eyes, preparing to strike out against the doctor. At the very last second, Dr. Conkle-Smoak found what he was looking for. He removed a hefty, horseshoe-shaped magnet from his pocket and hurled it with all his might at the leader of the wednesdays. Two grinned malevolently at the object as it flew toward him, clearly confident in his ability to thwart the missile. But then . . . THUD! The magnet made direct and solid contact, hitting Two squarely between the eyes and knocking him to the ground. Only then did Dr. Conkle-Smoak, braver than anyone had given him credit for, turn around and run as fast as his tangled, billowing robe allowed.

Max also turned to run, but he paused to look back one last time. Two sat on the ground, rubbing his head and shouting angrily at Three. The rest of the wednesdays looked bewildered. Relieved that they were focused on each other rather than on his friends, Max hurried away into the midnight shadows.

CHAPTER 29

Halfway up the steep slope of Mount Tibidabo, barely a minute into Wednesday, Max ran fast, but he did not run directly. Instead of heading straight to his backyard, he raced through the narrow, meandering streets of the Wednesday-darkened village. He wanted to keep running, farther and faster, until the clock's terrible message couldn't possibly reach him—if such a distance even existed. He ran until he could scarcely breathe, until his eyes stung from sweat and his leg muscles quivered. But the feeling still remained.

He *felt* Wednesday.

Or, perhaps it was more accurate to say that he felt *like* a wednesday. He wasn't certain how best to describe it. Whatever it was, he had felt it first while standing at the clock: a clear and awful calling when the clock struck twelve, as if something decidedly *not* Max was awakening within his body—and even more terribly, within his mind.

At that moment, the only thing that kept Max from running away forever was the knowledge that his friends stood waiting for him, exposed and vulnerable outdoors on a Wednesday. This, and only this, persuaded him to slow his pace and head toward his home.

His friends were waiting, wide-eyed and tense, and no one objected when Max insisted that they keep their meeting brief. "Two saw all of you, and he knows you were with me. He might try to harm one of you out of spite. You're better off indoors."

Noah was anything but scared, though. "Did you all see that? Did you see the teeth on the big one? Did you *smell* them? Geez, Max, I hope you don't start smelling like them. What do you think would happen if I shot one with my BB gun? Or, maybe we could dig a pit and put spikes at the bottom, or—"

Dr. Conkle-Smoak interrupted Noah's blabbering. "Settle down, lad. There'll be no guns or traps. I daresay they wouldn't work on these creatures anyway. Just look at these astral spectrometer readings—they're quite literally off the charts!" His measurement device was smoking slightly, and it smelled of melted plastic.

Gemma didn't look as scared as she ought to, either. But

she was uncharacteristically silent, and her pretty brow was furrowed in deep thought.

Max wanted to send them all home as soon as possible—especially if they didn't have the sense to fear for their own safety—but something was puzzling him. "Doctor, why did Two let that magnet you threw hit him in the head? Whenever I've thrown anything at a wednesday, it's always bounced right back and hit *me* instead."

Dr. Conkle-Smoak, the one member of the group who seemed properly frightened, looked pleased beneath his terror. "I was testing a theory, dear boy, and I do believe I may have stumbled upon something. You see, I have deduced the possibility that these wednesdays of yours have what parapsychologists refer to as an advanced psychic apparatus. In Freudian terms, you might say they have a pathological enlargement of the id. That, combined with their hyper-magnetized brain wave frequencies, makes them uniquely susceptible to—"

"Get to the point!" Max roared irritably.

"Fine," sniffed Dr. Conkle-Smoak, who looked hurt by Max's interruption. "To put it in the crass terminology that seems to be preferred by your appallingly inattentive generation: you need to shock the little slimeballs. Scorch 'em. Toast their nasty little toesies and make them dance like a kite in a windstorm. Zing. Zang. Poof. Am I making myself clear?"

Gemma arched one eyebrow as she and Max exchanged surprised glances, and even Noah was stunned into silence. The doctor now had everyone's complete attention.

"As I was saying," Dr. Conkle-Smoak continued, basking slightly in the newfound spotlight, "their abnormal magnetic fields appear to make them uniquely susceptible to electroshock."

Max gritted his teeth with impatience. He didn't understand half of what the doctor was rambling on about, but if the strange man had truly identified a wednesday weakness, then he had no choice but to let him continue.

"Let me show you what I mean." Dr. Conkle-Smoak rummaged around in his knapsack until he found what he was looking for. It was a crumpled and torn brochure that he smoothed down carefully on the patio table. Max had to squint to see it in the dim moonlight.

"It looks like a gun!" Predictably enough, Noah's interest was piqued.

"It's not a gun," the doctor chastised. "It is a state-of-the-art psycho-magnetic catabolizer. And it might just do the trick against these savage little buggers." He glanced apologetically at Max. "No offense to present company intended."

Max shrugged it off. "Where can we get one?"

"Well"—the doctor bit his lip nervously—"there's a slight question of legality, and it might take some time to get approved for an import license. I could ask around the occultist community, but they're a secretive bunch and not much inclined to share equipment."

Gemma hadn't said a word up until this point, but she was closely scrutinizing the brochure. "I've seen one of these before," she said softly, still thinking. Suddenly, her face lit up. "Yes! I know exactly where I've seen one. I think that I can get you one, Max, if you need it."

"Of course he needs it!" Noah answered for Max.

Just then, the lawn sprinklers turned on, instantly drenching the group with icy water. At the exact same time, Dr. Conkle-Smoak developed a vicious case of hiccups, and Gemma stubbed her toe painfully as she tried to escape the water from the sprinklers. Noah eyed Max suspiciously and took several large steps away from him.

Max stayed where he was, barely feeling the onslaught from the sprinklers. "Sorry, everyone," he apologized glumly, "but it *is* Wednesday, you know. You should all get inside before anything worse happens. I'll see you tomorrow."

They didn't need to be told twice; everyone hurried off in different directions. Dr. Conkle-Smoak hesitated and turned back toward Max. "I almost forgot to tell you. I think I know where they go when it isn't Wednesday."

Max sighed wearily. He was exhausted, and he didn't have the energy to listen to another one of the doctor's long-winded explanations. "Can you give me the quick version?"

The parapsychologist pulled a piece of paper out of his pocket; Max recognized it as the pencil rubbing that he had made from the words that he had found etched into the base of the clock tower. "I looked it up. *Psyche pannuchizein exodo* is Greek. Loosely translated, it means 'exit from soul sleep.'"

Max shook his head in frustration. "That makes no sense at all—it sounds like complete nonsense. For all we know, those words have nothing to do with the wednesdays."

Dr. Conkle-Smoak touched his shoulder gently, ignoring the water from the sprinklers even as it dripped into his eyes. "Max, it's a complicated concept, but it's one with a long and meaningful history. I believe they go into a dormant, transitional state of sorts—kind of a deep sleep, or hibernation, if you will—except on Wednesdays, when they are able to temporarily exit from the clock tower." He paused, looking as if he wanted to continue, but then stopped himself. "Speaking of sleep, young man, you look as if you need some yourself. Good night, Max."

As Dr. Conkle-Smoak hurried off into the night, Max crawled into his now-soggy tent. It was cold and miserable, but he didn't want to risk going in the house and ruining his parents' night. The sprinklers finally turned off, and Max pulled his damp sleeping bag around him, shivering slightly in the night air.

Maxwell V. Bernard. Next. One Hundred. *Wednesday*.

"Who am I?" Max asked aloud. But, of course, no one answered him. Pulling the sleeping bag up to his chin, Max contemplated the doctor's theory that the wednesdays were simply asleep the rest of the week. Could it be that simple? He struggled to recall what Ninety-eight had said. *"There's Wednesday, and then there's not-Wednesday. On not-Wednesdays, there are not wednesdays."*

Max didn't know what to think; he was too tired to even try. As he started to drift off, Ninety-nine's weak voice echoed in his mind. *Next week . . . next week . . . next week . . .*

He only had one week left.

CHAPTER 30

Max spent that Wednesday close to home. After all, he reasoned sadly, it could very well be his last Wednesday *ever* with his family. He spent the day playing canasta with his parents through the kitchen window. They had developed a system using sign language and note cards to communicate through the glass. When it was time to pass cards, Max's father would open the window just enough to squeeze the cards through the crack, one at a time. They made it through the afternoon with only a few minor incidents, although his dad did wind up with his eyeglasses broken and his sweater unraveled.

The family cat had long since learned to spend Wednesdays in deep feline hiding, but Max's mother assured him that its fur was growing back nicely.

Only baby Leland seemed to sense that something was

amiss. He absolutely insisted that his high chair be placed by the window so that he could press his face against the glass and watch Max's every move with wide, curious eyes. He didn't spit up or fuss once that afternoon, which in and of itself made it a most unusual day. Odder still, though, was the single syllable he babbled and cooed nearly constantly between his bottles and his diaper changes. "Neh, neh, neh," he repeated all day long.

"Listen, everyone! He's trying to say his first word," his mother shouted. "Say *Mommy*, Leland darling. *Mah-meeee*."

"Neh," said baby Leland.

Their voices were muted through the windowpanes, but Max could hear well enough to guess exactly what baby Leland was trying to say.

He was trying to say "Next."

Oh, certainly, it could have been "neck," or "nap," any one of a hundred nonsense syllables that all babies utter meaninglessly, but Max knew better. He stared back at his baby brother and wished he could speak. "What do you know?" he asked softly. But no matter how strongly Max tried to will his baby brother to reveal his secrets, Leland simply continued to stare and to cheerfully repeat his lone word fragment.

"Neh." Baby Leland smiled adoringly at Max. "Neh, neh, neh, neh."

At dinnertime Max's father moved the dining room table close to the window so that Max would feel as if he was sitting with them as he ate his meal on the back step. His mother waved at him cheerfully through the window and held up the pitcher of lemonade—her way of asking whether he wanted more.

"No, thank you," he mouthed.

As he ate, he sang the wednesday song in his head:

A wednesday's job is never done
As long as Wednesdays are.
We heed the clock when it tolls twelve
And come from near and far.
We're never late—we cannot be—
For then we'd miss the door.
Neither do we dare to leave
Till Wednesday is no more.

There was something important in the lyrics—he was certain of it.

As he pondered the meaning of the song, Max's thoughts wandered to something Ninety-nine had said. He said that Two had selected him six weeks ago. *Why then? Why me?* Max wondered. *What happened six weeks ago?*

And then he remembered.

It was such a minor incident that it was no wonder it hadn't occurred to him before. He counted backward on his fingers just to be sure. Yes—that had to be it. Exactly six Wednesdays ago he had been cooped up in the house as usual, going nearly mad with boredom. It was a stormy, dreary day, so Max had been delighted when the weather worked itself up into a dramatic electrical storm. Lightning was streaking vividly across the cloud-darkened sky, and the rain was coming down nearly sideways in the stiff wind. As he stood watching the storm from his bedroom window, Max had wanted to breathe in the fresh, charged feel of the lightning-scorched wind. He'd opened his window and inhaled the stormy air for only the briefest of moments before the rain had begun to splatter into his room. As he struggled to close the window to keep his carpet from getting soaked, he had noticed some sort of animal scurrying across the street. The creature was illuminated by a bolt of lightning just long enough to draw Max's attention, but not long enough for him to identify it. The next flash of lightning revealed only the empty street, so Max had forgotten all about it.

He now wondered if that scampering creature in the storm had been Two. Was it possible? Could a single, careless moment standing in the open window have cost him his humanity?

His mother startled him by tapping three times on the window—the signal that she was about to serve dessert. Max stood up and dutifully moved to the far side of the backyard long enough for her to quickly open the back door and slide a piece of banana cream pie out to him. He wrinkled his nose and then shuffled back to pick at it once the door was firmly closed; he had never much cared for cream pies. He glumly observed that the crust was burned—his fault somehow, no doubt.

He was picking the mushy banana chunks out of the cream filling when inspiration struck. Something about the round banana slices reminded him of the round clockface. He angrily squished the pieces of fruit with his fork, wishing he could squish the clock as easily . . . when he realized he might, in fact, be able to do just that. Or, at least something with the same end result. *If I sabotage the clock, the wednesdays will have no way to get out.*

The more he thought about it, the more it seemed possible. According to the song, the clock was the wednesdays' door. And Dr. Conkle-Smoak had said that the words engraved into the clock tower referred to an exit of some sort. If this was true, then perhaps destroying the clock would destroy their exit!

Max desperately wanted to share his theory with someone, but when he glanced through the window at his parents cozily feeding one another bites of pie, he just couldn't bear the thought of getting their hopes up if his plan didn't work.

He would simply have to wait until Thursday to talk to anyone.

CHAPTER 31

Max hardly slept a wink that night. He tossed and turned fitfully, and during the precious few moments when he finally did manage to drift off, he was haunted by bizarre dreams involving silver lightning bolts shooting out from storm clouds made of rotten banana cream pie. It was a thoroughly unpleasant night, but at least it had given him much-needed time to think.

By Thursday morning Max had come up with a plan that just might work. He was nearly bursting with the need to share it by the time a breathless Gemma showed up in his backyard at half past noon.

"I know, I know—I'm late, aren't I? Don't be angry with me, though; it wasn't my fault. That wretched Mrs. Trimersnide caught me sneaking off school grounds, believe it or not. I'd still be her prisoner if I hadn't threatened to publish a story in the school paper about her nasty little habit of swiping food out of students' lunch bags." Gemma grinned devilishly as she pulled something out of her backpack. "Anyway, look what I've got."

Max stared in amazement. "It's one of Dr. Conkle-Smoak's psycho-magnet thingies!" He couldn't even begin to imagine how Gemma had managed to find the small silver weapon, which looked like an odd sort of cross between a gun, a flashlight, and his father's electric shaver.

"Psycho-magnetic catabolizer," she corrected him. "Otherwise known to the rest of the world as a stun gun. When I saw the doctor's brochure, I was positive I had seen one before— it just took me a moment to figure out where."

Max reached out to touch the weapon, then hesitated. If it worked against wednesdays, then it might work against *him*. "Where did you get it?"

"Since he's the mayor, my father is also the village's deputy constable. He doesn't need a gun, since nothing truly dangerous ever happens here, but the chief constable gave him this, just in case." Gemma pressed a button and the device made a loud zapping noise as a blue electrical current sizzled and arced between two probes on the end of the weapon.

Max jumped back, startled. A burnt ozone smell wafted from the device.

Noah burst into the backyard just in time to see Gemma's demonstration. "Oh, cool! You got one of those wednesday zapper guns. Let me have a turn." He grabbed at the weapon.

Gemma, who was at least three inches taller than Noah, sighed and held the device out of reach. "All in good time," Gemma chastised him. She turned to show Max how the stun gun worked. "So, you just press this end against the wednesday and then hit this button. He'll get a nasty shock that he won't soon forget."

Max felt his stomach sink. He shook his head slowly. "I have to be close enough to touch them with it? It'll never work," he said. "Two's not about to let me get near enough to zap him."

"See, I *told* you we need a *real* gun," Noah whined.

"No!" Max and Gemma shouted him down in unison.

But as Noah sulked, an idea snaked its way into Max's mind. There *was* someone who could get close enough to the wednesdays to use the stun gun . . . someone who had plenty of experience with weapons.

He hopped to his feet. "I need to go ask someone for a favor. I'll meet up with you later." Max refused to tell them anything else until he knew that his plan would work.

• • •

Thursday snapped and growled murderously from the porch as Max approached the house. The tiny dog looked uglier than ever with his crooked teeth bared and his patchy fur standing on end. A string of saliva hung suspended from his mouth, and his pinkish, rheumy eyes were focused menacingly on Max.

Max took several nervous steps backward, certain that the snarling dog was about to attack. For such a tiny little animal, he seemed awfully vicious. Fortunately, Mr. Grimsrud pushed through the door just in the nick of time. "What's wrong, little fella?" He struggled to restrain the dog, who seemed singularly determined to eat Max.

"Well, now, that's curious," the old man said once he had wrestled the dog into the house. Thursday continued to bark wildly from behind the door. "He usually only gets like that when he smells a wednesday. Oh . . ." His voice trailed off as he noticed Max's gangly arms and large, silver eyes. "I see."

Max hung his head in shame. "I need your help," he whispered.

Mr. Grimsrud began knocking on the side of his head nervously before Max was even halfway through his explanation. By the time the old man heard what Max wanted, he was tapping an anxious SOS pattern into his skull. "I'm afraid that's simply not possible, young man. I'm truly sorry for your troubles, but I want no part of them. I have Thursday to think of, after all. You seem nice enough—at least when you're not covered in garbage. I'm sure you have plenty of friends who'd be willing to help out."

"But, Mr. Grimsrud, that's just it. *You* are the only person in the village they don't bother! You're the only one who can get close enough to use the stun gun," Max pleaded with him. "Please, sir, you're my last hope."

The old man shook his head. "I've always left them alone, and they've always left me alone. Doesn't make much sense to change anything about that."

It seemed like a lost cause, but Max gave it one last shot. "But weren't you a soldier?" he asked, as if he didn't already know the answer. "I mean, you fought in a *war*. These are just a bunch of short, funny-looking creatures—they don't carry guns or drive tanks. Honestly, what's the worst that can possibly happen?"

Mr. Grimsrud stopped knocking on his head and glowered irritably. Max could see he was hitting a nerve, so he pressed on. "You fought for your country; that's how you got the metal plate in your head, right? Well, this is like fighting for your village. Except you won't actually have to fight at all. Well, at least not really. You just have to zap them a little with a stun gun. It should be a piece of cake for a man with your . . . experience." Max was really laying it on thick, he knew, but he couldn't seem to stop himself.

A strange expression crept across Mr. Grimsrud's grizzled face, and for a moment Max feared he had blown his last chance completely. Then he realized that the old man actually appeared to be getting misty-eyed!

Max took a step back, confused. Anger, he could have understood—he might have pressed too hard and offended the old man. But . . . tears?

Mr. Grimsrud snuffled a bit and then dabbed at the corner of his eye with a frayed shirtsleeve. "I never dreamed I'd ever hear the call to duty ringing in my ears again," he whispered. And, although *technically* he hadn't said yes yet, a change came over him. He stood up straighter, with his shoulders back and his chest thrust forward. He snapped his heels together, rapped sharply once on his head, and saluted a flagpole in his yard that currently flew nothing but a bird's nest.

Max couldn't tell whether the old man had consented to help or not. "Shall I come by and get you late Tuesday night, then?" he asked hesitantly.

Seeming altogether oblivious to Max's continued presence, Mr. Grimsrud began to loudly hum the national anthem. Thursday howled in harmony from inside the house.

Max crept away, wanting very badly to hope that this meant yes.

CHAPTER 32

Max, who was feeling very much determined to *remain* Max, diligently set about learning all there was to know about clocks. He spent several entire days poring through a book on clock repair that he had found in the library, and he spent his sleepless nights feverishly sketching out charts, timelines, and intricate diagrams. Twice he even used Gemma's key to sneak into the tower to study the village clock's dials and levers. It was a complicated piece of machinery, but after days of studying and tinkering, he felt as if he finally understood enough to get the job done.

His original plan was to destroy the clock altogether. If the clock was demolished, then the wednesday door would stay shut forever. Or, at least that was what he *thought*. Aside from the nagging fact that the clock's destruction would likely require jackhammers, dynamite, or other such difficult-to-acquire supplies, it had seemed the most logical solution overall.

When he described his plan to Noah and Gemma, though, Noah was quick to point out the obvious problem with it. "Sounds like fun, but it won't work. They'll just fix it right up." He was pouring the last crumbs from a bag of chips into his mouth as he said it, and Max ignored him as he chewed with his mouth open.

"No, really—" Noah went on anyway, oblivious to the bits of food spraying out of his mouth as he spoke. Gemma glared as she flicked a wet clump off of her shoulder. "Everyone in this village is nuts about that clock. They'll never just let it sit around broken forever. My mother's even on the Tibidabo Clock Committee, you know? They hold a bake sale in the square every year to pay for the clock maintenance, and last year she stayed up for two nights in a row baking hundreds of cupcakes for it. Don't you remember when the whole village went berserk just because someone suggested replacing one of the old bells? The village priest and one of the aldermen almost got into a fistfight over it—one of them was going on and on about 'tonality' or 'musicality' or something, and the other, the one who tried to land a punch, kept yelling about 'historical value.'" Noah licked the salt from his fingers. "Nah, they'll just fix it if you break it."

Max sighed. Noah was probably right. The clock tower

was the centerpiece of the village, and people *did* get a bit goofy about preserving it.

After a great deal of discussion, much of which was monopolized by ridiculous suggestions from Noah that prominently featured gunpowder, storm troopers, or souped-up monster trucks, they finally agreed it would be better to just set the clock ahead, ever so slightly. The change would have to be small enough so that no one in the village would really notice, but big enough to make sure that it would discourage the wednesdays. And, judging from what they had seen of poor Ninety-nine's two minutes of Tuesday, it seemed highly likely that three, or four, or maybe even five minutes of Tuesday would most certainly get their attention.

"Maybe, but I'm still convinced that you've gone soft in the head," Noah grumbled. "Perhaps we should make them a nice cup of tea while we're at it?" He, of course, thought the plan sounded far too mild to be effective. But they had all seen Ninety-nine's miserable two minutes, so even Noah finally had to concede that it just might work.

"Think of it like an electric fence," Max argued. "If the clock is set early, then when it strikes midnight, the wednesdays will try to come through the door before it's actually Wednesday. In other words—they'll run right into the electric fence. And with any luck at all, Two'll be the first in line to get a nice big taste of Tuesday Surprise. He'll go running back into the clock faster than you can say 'yesterday.' We can start with five minutes, and tell them that we'll keep setting the clock earlier and earlier until they let me go."

The electric fence explanation cheered Noah considerably. "I can't wait to see the look on their ugly faces when they pop out and it's really still Tuesday. ZAP!" He dropped to the floor and writhed around in mock agony. "But shouldn't we start with more than five minutes?" he asked from his position on the ground.

Max frowned. He didn't want to be soft on the wednesdays, but he didn't want to *destroy* them, either. "Well, Two banished the girl wednesdays to not-Wednesday, and they haven't been seen in a hundred years. I don't know how long it takes until they just . . . vanish, or whatever it was that happened to the girls. Besides, five minutes feels like forever when you're suffering as much as Ninety-nine was." Max did not add the fact that *he* might soon enough be suffering right along with the wednesdays, but he thought it.

"Is that what happened to One?" Noah asked. "He was kicked out, too?"

Max nodded eagerly. "I'm almost sure of it. See? So they've done it at least twice. They made the girls *and* One disappear by forcing them into a day other than Wednesday. There's absolutely no way my plan can fail. They either agree to let me go, or else they risk vanishing like the girls and One."

Gemma, who had remained silent up until this point, scoffed loudly.

"What?" Max challenged her. The sleepless nights were wearing on him, and his patience was frightfully thin.

She sighed wearily. "Neither of you considered for a moment, did you, that One *was* a girl?"

Max and Noah both cocked their heads in identical expressions of confusion.

Gemma rolled her eyes. "So typical. What, you think girls can't be leaders? Welcome to the twenty-first century, boys. It's obvious, isn't it? One was a girl and Two kicked her out with the rest after a power struggle."

Max was embarrassed to admit it had never even crossed his mind that the original wednesday could be a girl. Two was just so ugly and awful that he couldn't even imagine a girl being even uglier or awful-er than him. "Okay, you're probably right, but that doesn't change the plan. We know Two made One disappear by banishing *her*, so he should be terrified of the same thing happening to him."

Gemma eventually nodded in agreement with the plan, but she looked skeptical.

"What now?" Max asked. He was starting to get a terrible headache, and he was half convinced that he could actually *feel* his head growing more and more squarish.

"Oh, nothing. I mean, I suppose it's the only way. . . ." She trailed off. "Whatever it takes, right?" But still, she frowned.

When Dr. Conkle-Smoak arrived, he was also unconvinced. He halfheartedly argued something about spacetime continuums and polar objectivity, but it quickly became clear that, for all his blathering and fancy words, he couldn't come up with anything better. "Well, at least be ready with the psycho-magnetic catabolizer, just in case you need it."

Max stared blankly at him for a moment until Gemma whispered "stun gun" discreetly into his ear. "Oh, right. That. I've already worked that into the plan, as a matter of fact. We'll have an expert of sorts helping out with that part."

Dr. Conkle-Smoak was visibly relieved that he hadn't been assigned any of the more dangerous roles in the plan. "But perhaps I ought to attend as an observer, so I can document everything for posterity."

"Oh, yes, and I'll have my video camera, too," Gemma said casually.

"What?" This was the first Max had heard about Gemma bringing a camera.

Gemma shuffled her feet sheepishly. "Well, why shouldn't I? It could come in handy . . . depending on how things turn out."

"Meaning, in case I vanish forever into wednesday oblivion? So you can prove that you 'knew me when' to help you become a famous television reporter?" Max was hurt, although he didn't quite know why. Even though he himself had wanted to bring a camera when he first met the wednesdays, now it just didn't seem *right*. Besides, he was becoming horribly self-conscious about his changing appearance, and the last thing he wanted was for his disturbingly square head and egg-shaped body to be captured on film for the whole world to see.

Gemma blushed and chewed on her lip; she at least had the good grace to look ashamed of herself.

Noah jumped to her defense, though. "Don't be a twit, Max—bringing a camera's a *genius* idea! How else will you prove that you got rid of the wednesdays forever? Having it on video will make you a hero, you lunkhead."

Max appreciated his best friend's enthusiasm, even if it was overly optimistic. "All right," he said quietly, suddenly feeling an intense need to be alone for a while. "I'll see you all tomorrow night."

● ● ●

Max needed air.

He decided to hike up the Mount Tibidabo trail, which wound steeply through the forested slopes above the village. He discovered that his new, bouncy, wednesday legs were faster than his old legs, and in no time at all he was hiking in wooded isolation with no signs or sounds of civilization anywhere. Normally he would have found it spooky, but at the moment it just felt peaceful. Besides, these days he was probably the spookiest creature in the forest anyway. If there were any wolves or bears to be found, then they were wise to stay out of his way. Come to think of it, the forest seemed strangely deserted. None of the usual nature sounds could be heard—there wasn't so much as a chirp, a rustle, or the snapping of a twig. *I really am the creepiest thing in the forest*, he thought. *I've scared everything else away.*

He kicked dejectedly at a fallen pinecone as he walked. Predictably enough, it ricocheted off a tree and hit him in the head. Max barely felt it. *What if I just keep going and never come back? If they can't find me, then maybe they can't turn me into a wednesday.* Running away was awfully tempting, but Max suspected it wasn't quite so simple as that. He had no choice but to confront the situation.

But something was troubling him as he hiked at his breathless pace. The image of Ninety-nine writhing in pain and screaming in agony kept playing over and over again in his mind. He wondered how long Ninety-nine had been a wednesday. It could have been weeks ago, or it could have been hundreds of years ago, but Ninety-nine had been, at some point, just a boy. A boy like Max.

Max suspected that Ninety-nine's transformation had

been a recent one, because in spite of his strange, wednesday appearance, there was still something unmistakably *human* in him. Ninety-eight still seemed to have a bit of his humanity left, too. He might have played pranks on Max, but Ninety-eight had never seemed malicious or cruel. He was actually sort of fun, Max thought grudgingly. Even Sixty-one and Sixty-two, who had likely been wednesdays for quite a long time, still had a brother-like bond left over from their previous lives. That was proof of *something*, Max recognized, but of what he still wasn't certain. If nothing else, it showed that the wednesdays weren't all bad. Or, at least that they weren't all bad all the time. They just *became* bad over time as their mind's mind, or whatever it was, took over the person they used to be.

As he hiked furiously up the slope, thinking these half-wednesday thoughts, Max came to a decision. He didn't yet know *how*, but he did know that his plan would have to change. The change could cost him everything, but it was the only way he could live with himself.

CHAPTER 33

Out of all the many, many other miseries caused by his case of the wednesdays, perhaps the saddest was that Max seemed to have lost his old sense of adventure. He spent his final Tuesday alone in his backyard, not doing much of anything. His case of the wednesdays was now strong enough that he could do nothing to prevent his contagious calamities, and he simply couldn't bear to spend what might be his very last day bringing bad luck to the people he loved.

So, he watched his family through the windows, feeling like a different species altogether from his mom and dad and little Leland. He watched as his father piggybacked the baby around the living room; his mother was clapping, and they were all smiling and laughing together. Leland spit up all over his dad's back, but not even that dampened their mood.

Then his mother caught sight of him standing outside,

looking in. The smile on her face wilted quickly, and Max watched as her eyes filled with tears. Baby Leland took his cue from Mommy and started to cry as well. Max's father looked down at his feet.

Max had ruined the moment. He'd ruined *everything*. His mother gestured at him to come inside, but Max shook his head, not sure that he could bear it.

He just couldn't bring himself to say goodbye.

His mother stuck her head out the back door to insist, though. "Maxwell, darling, you look so glum. Be a dear and put your little brother to bed, would you?"

"But what if something bad happens?" Max felt as if he was speaking through a lump in his throat.

"Oh, I think that we can manage with a few bumps and spills. Leland just adores you, you know. Let him have a few minutes with his favorite big brother." She smiled gently and held the door open.

Max could hardly refuse her, even if time was getting short. Noah and the others expected him at the clock tower in just a few minutes, but Max found himself nodding in agreement. *This can't possibly take long,* he reasoned.

• • •

As it turned out, it took *quite* a long time.

Baby Leland simply would not fall asleep. At first he

was perfectly well behaved, staring, mesmerized, at Max. He reached his little baby fingers up into Max's face, content to play with his reflection in Max's now undeniably silver eyes. He gah-gahed and goo-gooed happily—right up until the instant Max tried to move so much as an inch away from him. And then he screamed bloody murder, howling as if Max had meanly poked him with a pin.

Next, Max tried standing up with the baby in his arms. He mimicked the bouncing, dancing sort of steps he had seen his parents do so many times while trying to soothe Leland. But once again it was all good and fine right up until the moment that Max tried to set him back in his crib, and then the shrieking began anew.

"Hush, Leland. I don't have time for this!" Max pleaded in a whisper. But baby Leland would not be consoled.

Several times, Leland seemed to finally drift off to sleep. His eyes closed and he began to breathe in deep, rhythmic breaths that sounded like little sighs. But, yet again, the very instant Max tried to put him to bed, he jolted upright and howled so loud and long that Max began to worry his little lungs would run out of breath. Leland seemed positively determined not to let Max leave the room, almost as if he knew his brother's plan and was trying to prevent it.

Max glanced desperately at his watch. It was getting so late! He thought of simply plunking baby Leland in his crib and darting out the door, or calling in his mother or father for reinforcement, but he didn't. He couldn't bear to leave. Not while his baby brother was crying as if his heart would break. Max couldn't accept the thought of his little brother's wails being the last sound he ever heard from his family. From his home. So he rocked. And rocked. And whispered, and sang.

First he sang lullabies and whispered little made-up stories. Then, carried away by his own distracted thoughts, he leaned into baby Leland's ear and began to whisper his

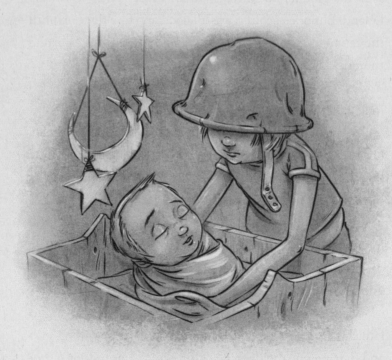

plan for dealing with the wednesdays. He whispered his doubts and his questions about the strategy, and he found himself sorting it out, bit by bit, even as he spoke. "All right, little brother. If you won't let me out of here in time to start Wednesday early, I suppose I'll just have to find another way," he said softly. "Let's see what we can come up with."

Finally, as Max's whispered plan came together, Leland quieted at last. He uttered one more gurgly coo of approval, slowly closed his long-lashed eyes, and fell soundly asleep. Max held his breath until he couldn't stand it for another second and then tiptoed out of the darkened room.

He did *not* say goodbye.

● ● ●

And so it was that Max waited until what could possibly be the last hour of the last Tuesday of his human life to gather his team and announce the change of strategy. He'd only just made up his own mind, while rocking baby Leland, and he didn't have much time to convince the others.

"*What?* Have you gone completely mad?" Noah's reaction was even stronger than Max had predicted. He'd been anxiously waiting for Max to show up for hours, and he was still sore at his best friend's vanishing act.

"Dear boy, I'm afraid you might be making a terrible mistake." Dr. Conkle-Smoak didn't like Max's new plan, either.

Only Gemma remained silent, but her eyes met Max's with a newfound respect. She smiled ever so slightly and nodded in approval.

"But, Max, if you're wrong—"

Max interrupted Noah. "If I'm wrong, I'll be a wednesday forever. Trust me, I know."

Max knew the stakes were high, but foolish or not, there was a part of him that was certain that the new plan would work. Or, at least mostly certain. Certain *enough*, anyway. Perhaps he was transformed enough that he was already thinking like a wednesday. Or, perhaps Noah was right and he'd already lost his mind. Whether it was the wednesday in him or just plain madness, he didn't know, but something was telling him that he was doing the right thing.

"It'll work. If we follow the old plan and set the clock so that it strikes early, then all of the wednesdays will suffer. But the youngest ones—the most innocent wednesdays—will suffer *more*. They're smaller and weaker. For all we know, Two might barely even be bothered by the pain of Tuesday. And just look at Three's ugly, scarred face—he looks as if he's been through much worse than a few minutes of Tuesday." Max was on a roll; he'd spent the last several hours thinking this over.

"And what if Two refuses to release me? Or, for that

matter, what if he *can't?* My transformation into a wednesday might be out of his hands. And where am I left then? Sure, you could keep setting the clock forward week after week, calling them earlier and earlier, but what good will that really do? They'll be tortured horribly, week after week, as they show up when it's still actually Tuesday. You all saw what happened to Ninety-nine during his two minutes of Tuesday—it was really, truly awful, wasn't it? Two may deserve it, and the rest of his Tribunal goon squad as well, but not all of the wednesdays are bad. They didn't ask to become wednesdays any more than I did. It's not fair to them. And if this doesn't work out, it's not fair to me, either." Max's voice dropped to a near whisper. "That could be me next week, suffering perhaps worse than any of them."

Noah was still shaking his head, but Max quickly explained the new plan before anyone could interrupt him. It wasn't the least bit complicated: instead of setting the clock ahead, he would simply set the clock five minutes *late*. "Think about the words from their song: *We're never late— we cannot be, for then we'd miss the door.* So, if the clock strike is what calls them to the door, then when the clock is late, they'll miss the door. They'll be trapped inside. They won't have to suffer any Tuesday torture, and they won't be able to come out to complete my transformation." He gulped and tried to sound braver than he felt. "At least, I hope not."

"But how late is 'late,' Max? What if five minutes isn't

enough? Why not an hour? Or three hours?" Noah refused to be convinced. "Besides, who cares if they suffer? They bloody well deserve it for everything they've done to you—and for everything they do to the village every Wednesday! You don't owe them anything. Well, except maybe revenge. Let's march up the clock tower right this second and sound the bells. Let 'em suffer until they agree to let you go!"

But Max refused to change his mind. "My plan will work," he said firmly. *It had to*.

"Then I'm coming into the clock tower with you," Noah insisted.

"Me too," Gemma chimed in, already starting to adjust the light settings on her camera.

Dr. Conkle-Smoak shuffled his feet and busied himself with a piece of lint on his sleeve. "Um, er, I suppose that I could come in with you . . . if it's absolutely necessary, er, I mean, if I can be of assistance." Beads of sweat broke out on his upper lip. "I have magnets," he said weakly, pointing to his bulging pockets.

"No." Max was firm. "You've all done enough. I can't protect you in there, and I don't want anyone else becoming like *me*." His friends winced when he said this. "There are only two of us they can't destroy. Me, because it's already too late for me, and Mr. Grimsrud because . . . well, I'm not sure exactly.

"Speaking of Mr. Grimsrud"—Max glanced at the time—"I'll be right back. I have to go fetch him."

The others looked up at the clock nervously. It was almost 11:30. They only had a half hour to wait until Wednesday, and—although none of them actually said the words out loud—to say goodbye.

• • •

On his way to Mr. Grimsrud's cottage, Max once again wondered if he should go back home and say a proper farewell to his family. *Just in case.* But he still couldn't bear to do it. He simply hadn't been able to bring himself to tell his parents that this might be his last Tuesday ever as their son. They had watched his physical transformation, of course—they knew he was less and less himself every day. His mom spent half her days lately making long-distance calls to so-called specialists in faraway places. But his parents did not know that this might be the end of Max and the beginning of One Hundred. In fact, right now, with less than thirty minutes until his fate was determined, they thought he was sleeping safely in his tent in the backyard.

Max hoped to be back long before they woke up, with the whole nightmare behind him. He had left a note on his pillow, though, just in case things went badly. It had taken him two days to write, and even now it seemed lacking. *How do you say goodbye forever?* He knew that his written words were not nearly enough, and he hoped that no one else would ever have to read his letter.

Max approached the cottage cautiously, in case Thursday was loose. Fortunately, the dog was inside the house, but he sensed Max before he could even raise his hand to knock on the door. The weather-worn door rattled frightfully as the dog flung himself against it over and over again, barking and growling furiously.

Suddenly, the commotion stopped. There was silence for a brief moment, but then the dog—who was now even angrier and more vicious than Max had ever seen him—reappeared in the picture window that faced the front yard. He lunged frantically, cracking his head against the glass panes, covering them with a thick saliva foam. Max began to back away, fearful that the crazed dog might actually break through the window.

Luckily, Mr. Grimsrud showed up before that happened. He told Max to wait while he led the snarling dog into a back room, offering an apologetic pat on the head to his loyal pet as he locked him away safely.

When the old man finally came to the door, Max took a step back in surprise. Mr. Grimsrud was dressed in a formal military uniform. His entire chest was covered in badges, ribbons, and medals, and his shoes were polished to a brilliant shine.

"Wow," breathed Max. "I had no idea."

Mr. Grimsrud knocked sharply once on his head; but this time the gesture almost looked like a salute. "Now, just give me a moment to find Thursday's leash and we'll be on our way. . . ."

"No, Mr. Grimsrud," Max exclaimed. "Thursday can't come with us. Didn't you see how he reacted when I showed up? He wants to kill me!"

"Thursday comes everywhere with me," the old man said firmly. "If he can't come, then neither will I."

Max groaned and checked his watch. He didn't have time to waste on arguments or delays. "Please, Mr. Grimsrud," he begged. "It's only for a little while. And just think— after tonight, you'll be able to buy your newspaper and go to the cafe on Wednesdays, because there won't be any more wednesday problems in the village," he said. "Hopefully," he added under his breath.

Mr. Grimsrud grumbled and cursed, but he finally relented. "I'm sorry about this, little fellow," he called back into the house. "I'll be back soon, and I'll make us a nice plate of corned beef hash to share."

They could hear the dog's enraged howls all the way back to the clock tower.

CHAPTER 34

Back at the clock tower, the full moon glowered down impatiently upon Max and his friends.

Noah, Gemma, and Dr. Conkle-Smoak had been busy. They had used an old wheelbarrow, a stack of cement blocks, the inner tube from a bike tire, and some long wooden planks to assemble a rickety cata-pult at the base of the tower. "We've been practicing our aim," Noah said proudly. "We're actually pretty good."

Max smiled weakly at the con-traption. It was a nice thought, but he didn't have the heart to tell his friends it would probably just backfire on them if they used it against the wednesdays. He handed

Mr. Grimsrud the stun gun and quickly introduced him to the rest of the group.

"Max?" asked Gemma. "Are you sure that you don't want me to come in with you? It only takes two people to work the catapult."

Max shook his head and gestured to her video camera. "No, you were right. You should stay out here where it's safer and record this." He didn't want to say it out loud, but they were all thinking the same thing: Gemma should capture the night's events just in case Max was never seen again. "I want you to document that I went into the tower as *myself. . . .*" He gulped. "And the people in the village should see who—or what—comes back out.

"Well, it's now or never, I suppose." He took a deep breath and held the door of the clock tower open for Mr. Grimsrud. "Shall we?"

"No, lad. After you. You're leading this mission, after all. I'm just along for backup." The old man propped the door open ceremoniously, then stood at attention and waited for Max to enter the tower first.

"Good luck," Gemma said softly.

"Blast 'em to bits and send them away forever!" Noah's farewell was as expected.

Dr. Conkle-Smoak bowed slightly, a solemn expression on his face. He placed an elaborate turban that he had made from tinfoil onto his head in preparation. "Just in case, Max. Just in case," he explained in response to Max's questioning glance.

Max inhaled deeply and glanced at the clock. It was 11:51. "Let's go," he said, and entered the tower.

• • •

Max reached the top of the spiral staircase. He looked back to see that Mr. Grimsrud was struggling several stories below him and was wheezing badly. "Oh, no," Max groaned out loud. They didn't have time for this!

He rushed back down the stairs to give the old man a hand. He tried not to act impatient, but he could feel his heart thumping anxiously in his chest. "Just a few more steps, Mr. Grimsrud. We really need to hurry, please."

"You're going to give me a heart attack, you whipper-snapper. Settle down—we'll get there in due time." Mr. Grimsrud seemed to be moving in slow motion, and his face was a worrisome shade of plum.

When they finally reached the top, it was 11:57. *Only three more minutes until Wednesday.*

Max rummaged through his pockets to find the diagram he had copied out of his library book; it showed how to adjust the time of the clock. Max had been dismayed to learn that changing a clock tower's time was far more complicated than changing the time on a watch or a regular alarm clock. In fact, the huge clock's mechanism, with all of its dials, gears, pendulums, and weights, looked to him as complex as a rocket engine. He had studied the diagrams enough, though, that he thought he could get the job done.

The clock was open-faced, and in maneuvering his way around the tower's bulky machinery, Max found himself standing in what was essentially an open window crisscrossed by the filigreed metal clock hands that were as thick as his leg and nearly as long as he was tall. From where he stood, behind the clock's elaborate face, the timepiece was backward, as if he were looking at it in a mirror. Max glanced down at his friends, waiting in the village square far below, and suffered a staggering blow of vertigo.

"Afraid of heights, lad?" Mr. Grimsrud was already in a firing stance, his feet shoulder width apart and the stun gun held out in front of him like a pistol. His breathing had returned to normal, and he looked very much the soldier. Max was suddenly intensely grateful for his presence.

"A—a bit, yes," Max stammered. He forced himself to turn his back to the window, and he commanded his muscles to stop their quivering.

He turned his attention to the gears in front of him, comparing them to the picture in the clock repair manual.

He had studied the clock before but never actually changed the time, not wanting to draw suspicion. He located what his book called the drive plate, which looked sort of like a simple clockface, complete with numbers inscribed on the metal surface. Sixty holes were drilled through the metal plate—one for each minute of the hour. With one last glance at the diagram, Max held his breath and reached for the spring-loaded pin that would enable him to rotate the plate that controlled the clock's minute hand. He simply needed to rotate the pin back five holes for the clock to move back five minutes.

Just as his sweating fingers gripped the pin and prepared to pull it from its locked position, though, Max heard a loud, metallic THUNK that sounded ominously similar to a gun being cocked. He froze, knowing from his careful readings of the clock repair book that this was what clockmakers called the clock's "warning," and that it indicated the strike mechanism had already begun to run. *He had to stop it.*

Max felt the blood rush from his head as the gears began to rotate, pulling the large strike hammer back in preparation for the clock to strike the hour. He looked at the clock in disbelief. It was only 11:59; he should have another full minute left!

With his heart pounding in his ears, he suddenly remembered from his studies that some clocks begin their complicated strike process in advance so that the first chime is poised to sound exactly on the hour. *He was too late!*

He frantically pulled the pin and rotated the heavy minute plate back five slots anyway, hoping to at least delay the strike. Nothing happened for a split second, and Max briefly believed he had actually managed to move the clock back in time to prevent the chime. As he eased the pin into the correct opening, though, the movement triggered something deep and disastrous within the clock.

The strike hammer released.

GONG went the deafening first stroke.

GONG went the heartbreaking second stroke.

"No!" Max screamed out as he grabbed desperately at the spinning, fanlike piece of metal that had started the whole process. *The strike governor,* his diagram called it, and he held on to it as if his life depended on it.

The spinning piece was awkwardly situated deep in the clock's mechanism, and it was vibrating and whirling as if it had a life of its own. Max braced himself, elbow-deep in gears and levers, and held on tight. He was vaguely aware of a sensation of wetness; he looked down to see blood dripping from a gash on his hand. But he felt no pain as he clung desperately to the clock parts. He knew that this was his last chance.

CHAPTER 35

Silence.

At least for the moment, there were no more gongs—Max had successfully stopped the clock from completing the rest of its strikes.

But he knew from his clock manual that once he let go of the metal strike apparatus, the clock would finish its chimes—the very chimes that would determine his fate. He tightened his grip and blinked rapidly as a trickle of sweat dripped into his left eye.

Even as Max held on, a sickly green glow began to fill the clock tower. With his ears still ringing from the strikes, it took him a moment to notice a buzzing sound growing louder and louder all around him. Max looked up into the tall rafters of the clock tower's spire. The buzzing was coming from the wasps' nest! Woken either by the chiming of the clock's bells or by the looming presence of the wednes-days, wasps began streaming out of the nest.

"Watch out!" Max shouted to Mr. Grimsrud to warn him about the danger. It quickly became apparent that he needn't have bothered, though, since the wasps were no threat to them. The insects fled their nest and hurriedly flew out of the tower in a single, buzzing mass. *They're running away from the wednesdays*, Max realized. He was grateful that he hadn't been stung, but the fact that the wasps feared the wednesdays enough to flee their snug nest in the middle of the night brought Max to an entirely new level of panic.

The air thickened and darkened around him, and for a moment Max thought the wasps had swarmed back into the tower. He closed his eyes, bracing himself for a sting.

When no sting came, he slowly looked up and then gasped. Before him was a blurry, shifting figure. It took him a moment to realize that it was Two, materializing before his very eyes.

As the clock's internal gears and levers turned, they seemed to be literally churning Two out of the clock's mech-anism. Deeper in the clock's innards, Max could see several more figures emerging from between the gears. The rotten, swampy smell of the wednesdays struck his nose, and Max recoiled, nearly losing his grip on the strike wheel.

Two's eyes were closed as he emerged, and he was

hunched over in fetal position as his appearance changed from a barely perceptible fog to a more solid form. He seemed to smell Max, though, because his nose twitched and wrinkled as if he had sniffed something tantalizing. His silver-gray eyes popped open in response. It took a moment for his bleary vision to focus, but once it did, his fanged mouth drew up into an evil, masklike grin. "Next," he mouthed. No sound left his lips, but Max knew exactly what he had said nonetheless. Two coughed violently, clearing his throat, and a sticky spray of putrid phlegm hit Max's face. "Welcome to Wednesday," Two croaked, his voice sounding as if it was being filtered through a century's worth of cobwebs, dust, and rot.

The creature's torso was already half visible when Mr. Grimsrud aimed the stun gun. "Halt!" the old man ordered. To Max, his voice and his uniform conveyed an impressive sense of authority. Two, however, began to laugh hysterically.

"You're no threat to us, you pathetic fool," Two mocked. "Without your ugly animal friend, we can destroy you." His laugh sounded like a cross between a rusty hinge being forced open and an animal being slaughtered; the terrible sound made Mr. Grimsrud falter and then take a hesitant step back. "Thursday," he whispered, finally understanding why he and he alone had walked about unscathed on

Wednesdays. It had nothing to do with the plate in his head—it was because of his dog! But Thursday was at home, locked up alone and miserable.

The old soldier recovered quickly from his surprise and lunged bravely at Two with his weapon raised. He pressed the stun gun against Two's contorted neck and pulled the trigger. A violent bolt of electricity surged around Two, illuminating the tower with a vivid light so white it was almost blue. Two's mouth opened as if he were shrieking silently, and his back arched while his long fingers twitched and flailed about in a terrible sort of spastic, electric jig. For the briefest of moments it looked as if Dr. Conkle-Smoak was right, and Two *could* be fought with an electrical shock.

But then Two raised his twitching arms above his head in a monstrous gesture of triumph, and the hateful grin on his face grew wider and even more hideous. Rather than injuring the wednesday, the stun gun had given him *more* strength and *more* energy.

"You're too late to stop it, Max. *You. Are. Next.*" Max watched helplessly as Two braced his hands against the clock's cogs and wheels and began to pull himself out of the machinery. *He was nearly out.* Three was also now fully visible, and he appeared to be using his considerable strength to push Two farther into the open. More and more wednesdays were beginning to emerge every second, their gangly limbs twisted and tangled in the clock gears. The straining, writhing cluster looked like a gruesome, breathing knot—part machine, part monster—with a hundred sinister, silver eyes.

Two had almost completely emerged from the clock's machinery when Max realized that something was holding him back. Somehow, from deep, deep within the clock, someone's thin, pale fingers were wrapped around Two's hairy wrist, pulling him down!

Two slashed viciously at the fingers with the weapon-like claws on his free hand, but he couldn't seem to free himself from the grip of his unseen captor. The angry creature raised his head and let out an unworldly scream of fury and effort. He managed to make another inch of progress out of the clock, but his assailant held tight and emerged from the cogs right along with him.

It was Ninety-eight!

Never had Max been so happy to see a wednesday. In spite of the chaos and Two's violent thrashing about, Ninety-eight grinned at Max, his squarish face as cheerful as ever. As Two battled savagely against his grip, Ninety-eight called out above the mayhem: "It's not too late, Max. You have until the last strike of the clock!"

Three jumped into the fray, pummeling Ninety-eight viciously, and the smaller creature disappeared from view. Suddenly, the mass of wednesdays shrieked collectively as Mr. Grimsrud lunged at them in a surprise attack with a crowbar that he had found lying in a corner of the clock tower. Two easily thwarted his assault with barely a glance, though, and the old man went tumbling.

Max froze in place. He couldn't flee or even hide, since he knew that if he let go of the clock, it would resume striking and seal his fate. He would be a wednesday—forever. He watched helplessly as Mr. Grimsrud crumpled to the ground. Max felt the will to fight draining out of him. *It's over*, he thought. He began to release his grip on the clock's strike wheel when suddenly, out of the corner of his eye, he detected a blur of motion.

At the precise moment that Mr. Grimsrud's body hit the wooden floor of the clock tower's upper level, a small streak appeared, seemingly from out of nowhere.

Thursday! Max had never thought he could be so happy to see the ugly dog, who had somehow managed to escape from the house to follow his beloved master.

The dog's small size and sickly appearance proved to be quite misleading. He attacked Two with the strength and viciousness of an entire army of guard dogs. Growling fiercely, he lunged and sank his crooked teeth enthusiastically into Two's shoulder.

Two shrieked and tried desperately to pull the dog off. But Thursday's jaws were as strong as steel, and Two's efforts only succeeded in allowing the dog to get a firmer grip.

It was almost enough.

Almost.

Even in his obvious agony, Two continued to climb out of the clock. Thursday thrashed and tore, but Two kept climbing. The creature was unstoppable.

Max glanced out the window of the clock tower in a panic, wishing now that his friends were by his side. They were far below and couldn't see what was happening, but they could still help.

"Now!" Max cried at the top of his lungs, hoping, frantically hoping that his friends would hear him and, against all odds, that the catapult would work.

In response, a small object flew in at tremendous speed, narrowly missing Max's head.

THUD.

Two shrieked so loudly and with such rage that Max longed to cover his ears. The whole tower shook with the noise, and it felt as if the sound would tear him apart from the inside out. He maintained his grip on the clock gears, though.

Another object whizzed by Max's nose.

"Duck, Max!" a voice yelled out from below at the same instant as Max heard another wonderfully, beautifully solid THUD.

He looked out the window again and his heart soared as he saw what was happening below.

Dr. Conkle-Smoak and Noah were launching magnets with the catapult. Any other kind of projectile probably would have backfired. But—magnets! The magnets came soaring into the clock tower as his brilliant friends launched one after the other.

And either their aim was impossibly good or else the magnets were drawn naturally to Two, because both shots so far had been direct hits. Max ducked just in time for a third magnet to whiz by.

THUD.

Another direct hit, this time to Three.

The magnets were working! They actually seemed to be driving the wednesdays backward.

Two, who already looked dazed, stumbled as Three panicked and fled back into the clock.

Thursday watched this happen, sneering in a most undoglike manner. Evidently, he smelled wednesday weakness.

The small dog attacked again with such viciousness that Two seemed to literally shrink back into the clock gears, trying to escape the onslaught.

Two's silver eyes turned black with pain as the dog bit him again and again, and he was no longer pulling himself out of the clock's machinery. In fact, Max realized that the wednesdays were fleeing with such haste that the gears were now actually turning *in reverse* as the creatures rushed back into the depths of the clock. The clock's hands weren't moving backward, though. The only thing that seemed to be moving was the main gear shaft, which was slowly sucking Two, along with the rest of the wednesdays, back into wherever—or whenever—it was they had come from.

"How does it feel?" Max couldn't help but shout out at Two, who continued to hiss at him as he struggled. "How do you like it when someone else controls your fate? Now you know how One felt when you banished her."

The other creatures began to fade away gracefully as the clock gears pulled the still-shrieking Two steadily down until only his shoulders and head were visible. Max expected Thursday to loosen his grip on the wednesday, but the dog's fury and loyalty apparently outweighed his sense of self-preservation, and he never let go, not even as he was being dragged into the clock's gears himself.

Just before Two's terrible screams faded away completely, Max heard several other voices floating upward from deep within the retreating green fog:

"Goodbye, Max."

"Thank you."

The voices were so faint that he couldn't really be sure who had spoken. Nevertheless, Max felt certain it was Ninety-eight and Ninety-nine bidding their farewells. "Go in peace, friends," Max whispered.

• • •

The clock tower was eerily silent.

Max wanted to run to Mr. Grimsrud, who was still lying unconscious in the corner of the tower, but he knew he had to maintain his grip on the clock's strike wheel for a few more minutes just to be sure. *Get up,* he silently willed the old man. *Get up!*

He didn't know how long it had been; he had lost all track of time. Every second seemed to last an eternity, but once he felt that at least five minutes had surely passed, he let go of the strike wheel and rushed over to the crumpled figure.

GONG! GONG! The clock hammered out the remaining ten strikes as soon as Max let go. The clock's face read midnight, but by Max's calculations, it was actually 12:05. *Let it be long enough,* he pleaded silently. *Let the door be closed.*

Mr. Grimsrud's eyes fluttered open as Max knelt down, and the old man waved him away irritably. "I'm fine, I'm fine. Can't an old man be left in peace to take a little nap now and then?" He pulled himself to his feet stiffly, but seemed no worse for the wear.

They both looked around the clock tower, wide-eyed. The clock had finished its strikes, and no more wednesdays had appeared. *Had it worked?*

"Hey, what's happening up there?" Noah's voice floated up from where he waited outside. "Is everyone all right?"

Max poked his head out the clockface and flashed a thumbs-up. The group below cheered loudly.

As Max helped Mr. Grimsrud make his way slowly down the spiral staircase, he described what Thursday had done. "I'm really very sorry about your dog," Max said solemnly.

The old soldier was quiet for a moment. "It's all right," he said finally, blinking back tears. "It's what he would have wanted. He finally got his wednesday."

CHAPTER 36

In the village square, just below the silent clock, stood five friends, old and new.

At first, none of them could speak.

Max couldn't stop trembling. His hand was cut badly from the clock, and he found that he didn't have the words to describe what had happened in the tower.

Noah stood frozen, dumbstruck, with his mouth half open.

Gemma's camera hung uselessly at her side.

Dr. Conkle-Smoak scratched his head and pulled at his ears, looking quizzically at Max, but asking nothing.

A single, solitary tear coursed down Mr. Grimsrud's wrinkled face.

Finally, Max found his voice. "Am I . . . ," he began in a croak. "Am I . . . me?"

His friends looked at him, seeming quite unsure themselves.

"I think so," whispered Gemma.

"I know so," said Noah in a voice quiet and confident. "Don't ask me how, but I can tell."

Dr. Conkle-Smoak nodded. "Yes, yes, I believe he's right. I believe you're you, though I can't prove it just yet."

Mr. Grimsrud knocked sadly on his head.

Max hesitated, not knowing how the group would respond to his next request. "This might seem strange, but I feel as if we should, I don't know, say a few words or something?"

Gemma agreed. "Yes, let's."

And so, in turn, each of them spoke a few quiet words.

Max simply thanked each of his friends by name, ending with those who couldn't hear. "Thank you, Ninety-eight, and thank you, Ninety-nine. For your friendship, your wisdom, and your sacrifice. We won't forget you. And thank you, Thursday, of course. You were braver than all of us combined."

Dr. Conkle-Smoak mumbled and cleared his throat. "Amazing. Simply amazing," he finally said, and left it at that.

Gemma was next. "I . . . I don't know that I have the words. There are so many mysteries. So many questions. I started off just chasing a story, but it turns out that some things are more important." She shook her head and then looked straight at Max. "I'm just glad you're here. I'm glad you're all right." She leaned over and gave Max a quick kiss on the cheek, causing *both* of them to blush slightly.

Noah kept it simple. "Goodbye forever, wednesdays. And welcome back, Max." He glanced protectively at his friend.

Mr. Grimsrud snuffled and wiped roughly at his eyes before he used his turn to say goodbye to Thursday. "You were the best friend a man could have," he said softly. "I'll miss you, little guy."

And then they all stood silently, under the watchful moon, listening to the silence.

● ● ●

Max crept into his tent in the backyard. After retrieving the goodbye letter that he had left for his parents and ripping it into tiny pieces, he tiptoed into the house and fell soundly asleep in his own bed.

He ran straight for the mirror when he woke up the next morning. Just as he had hoped, his old pants once again fit him perfectly, and his eyes had almost gone back to their original shade of light brown. *I'm me again.* He smiled into his reflection.

He hesitantly entered the kitchen, where his parents were trying to feed mashed-up waffles to baby Leland. They looked startled to see him, and his father quickly moved the syrup bottle out of reach before anything unlucky could happen to it. None of them said a word, but Max and his parents each seemed to be holding their breath.

It was baby Leland who spoke first. *"Mass,"* he said cheerfully. Max waited, needing to hear it one more time before he could truly believe it. *"Mass!"* Leland shouted in his burbly baby voice. He flung a fistful of waffle paste at Max's head to emphasize his point.

Max! He was saying Max! *Definitely* not Next.

He. Was. Max.

He and his parents all let out their breath in three separate, relieved whooshes, and Max ruffled his baby brother's hair affectionately. "Waffle, Maxwell?" his mother asked, still sounding slightly nervous, but smiling nonetheless.

Max grinned as he pulled up a chair next to baby Leland and dug happily into a wonderfully accident-free breakfast.

EPILOGUE

Tourists flocked from near and far to attend the Mount Tibidabo Wednesday Fair. The weekly event had become quite the attraction, with its live music, food stalls, and midday parade, complete with special daytime fireworks. Mr. Fife's woodwork shop still sold plenty of carved butterflies, but his more recent creations were far more popu-

lar: elaborately carved wooden figures that looked sort of like young boys, but with exaggerated limbs, funny egg-shaped torsos, and large, square heads. The eyes were crafted from small bits of mirror that reflected the image of whoever held the wooden figure.

Mothers tended to find them a bit creepy, but children adored them, and Mr. Fife sold staggering numbers of the wooden dolls.

Visitors to the village were immediately struck by the charming, one could even say unnaturally perfect, setting. But there was one small flaw that occasionally caught the attention of particularly observant tourists. Fortunately, Mayor Swift knew just how to deflect the criticism.

"Mayor, Mr. Mayor," called one such hawk-eyed tourist, whose family was busily devouring Tibidabo Wednesday Sundaes, a gooey ice cream treat sold by the village confectionery. "Pardon me, Mr. Mayor. Your town's clock is quite beautiful, but I can't help but notice that it's not keeping the correct time. In fact, it is *quite* inaccurate. It's at *least* five minutes slow." He frowned as if this troubling blemish was somehow ruining his vacation experience.

"Very observant of you." Mayor Swift smiled with a practiced manner. "You've just stumbled onto one of our village's claims to fame. Welcome to what we like to call Tibidabo Time. It's our own little local time zone."

The mayor pointed to a nearby craft stall that was selling T-shirts and coffee mugs emblazoned with a logo that read HAVE A GREAT TIBIDABO TIME, with a winking, silver-eyed smiley face underneath. The mayor exchanged a knowing glance with the T-shirt seller as the tourist gestured to indicate that he'd like to buy some of the souvenir items.

"Clever marketing gimmick," said the tourist, satisfied with the explanation.

The village's Wednesday Bagpipe Brigade began to play, and the mayor wandered off to ensure that the rest of the day, like all Wednesdays now in the village, was nothing short of perfect.

And the lovely little town *was* perfect—at least as far as tourists were concerned. Many of them left only reluctantly as the sun set and their children began to yawn and fuss. "You really should open an inn here. Your town needs a hotel," the visitors often commented, even as the villagers subtly steered them back into their cars and buses, helpfully pointing out the quickest route back to the city below. Ignoring the well-intentioned suggestions, the villagers just nodded and waved farewell, never mentioning that an inn of any sort would be a *disastrous* idea.

An inn, you see, would mean that outsiders could stay the night.

And to stay the night in the lovely, otherwise perfect little town, halfway up the slope of Mount Tibidabo, would be to hear the clock strike midnight.

And every night at the stroke of midnight, the clock's toll was accompanied by an ominous chorus of voices. The song they sang, although brief, was both sweet and wicked, and mocking and melancholy, all at the same time. Soft and threatening, the voices sang out:

> **Wednesdays come and wednesdays go,**
> **But we know something you don't know. . . .**

And each night at that same moment, the villagers shivered a little in their beds, or tiptoed downstairs to double-check the locks on the doors. It really was a perfect little town, they told themselves, even as they glanced about nervously.

And it *was* nearly perfect.

Nearly.

JULIE BOURBEAU has lived a life that is probably more adventurous than necessary. She has jumped out of airplanes, has been swept out to sea, and was married on a Himalayan mountaintop by Tibetan monks. When she grew weary of a lifestyle that required so many vaccinations, she decided to become a writer so that her characters could continue her adventures while she stayed safe and warm. She still travels (just not as far), now in the company of her two young sons, who in one way or another inspire all of her tales.

Julie's second novel, *King of Nowhere,* will be available in 2014. To learn more about Julie and her work, you can visit her on the Web at Julie-Bourbeau.com.